ANGEL DUST

Feathers and Fire Book 11

SHAYNE SILVERS

ARGENTO
PUBLISHING

CONTENTS

Shayne Silvers

Angel Dust

Feathers and Fire Book 11

A TempleVerse Series

ISBN 13: 978-1-947709-76-8

© 2021, Shayne Silvers / Argento Publishing, LLC

info@shaynesilvers.com

ASHES, ASHES, THEY ALL FALL DOWN...

A ngels are falling from the sky.

Heaven and Hell walk the streets.

The Four Horsemen have declared Callie Penrose a criminal.

Everyone is holding their breath, waiting for someone to flick the first domino...

Everything is about to change.

Shayne Silvers
WORDSLINGER AUTHOR

DON'T FORGET!

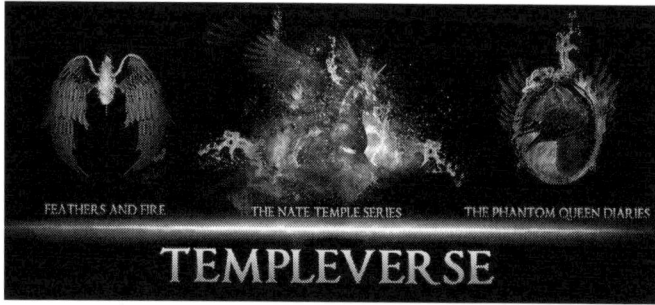

VIP's get early access to all sorts of book goodies, including signed copies, private giveaways, and advance notice of future projects. AND A FREE NOVELLA! Click the image or join here:
www.shaynesilvers.com/l/219800

FOLLOW and LIKE:
Shayne's FACEBOOK PAGE:
www.shaynesilvers.com/l/38602

I try my best to respond to all messages, so don't hesitate to drop me a line. Not interacting with readers is the biggest travesty that most authors can make. Let me fix that.

I

I sprinted down the dark hallway, panting and snarling like a beast. I wanted to taste my foe's blood on my tongue, to feel that tickling warmth slide down my throat, and the familiar waves of power rocking through me as my body responded to the magical nourishment it now craved.

I was Master Dracula, and no one survived invading my home.

No one.

My foe's silhouette came into view and I leapt forward with my claws outstretched. My jaws spread wide as my fangs extended in a silvery flash. Time slowed as my foe turned to face me and I caught my first look at the face of my evening meal.

A woman.

A beautiful, blonde-haired woman. I knew her. I had known her my entire life. She was my best friend.

Claire Stone.

She looked at me with a sad smile and haunted eyes, accepting her fate as the monster sailed directly towards her throat with the intent to kill.

No!

I didn't want to kill my best friend. I would *never* kill my best friend.

STOP! I screamed in my head.

But my body did not stop. It did not obey me. I was merely along for the ride, trapped inside the monster I had become.

Claire's lips moved in a silent message. *Sorry...*

My silver claws slammed into her chest as the full force of my weight brought her down to the ground and I arched my back to sink my fangs into her neck, all the while screaming *NO!* in my head.

My best friend's blood hit my tongue and my eyes rolled up into my skull as power arced through me like an electric current. Claire's warm body slowly went limp and Master Dracula continued to feed.

Inside, Callie Penrose was wailing and gnashing her teeth.

I pulled back, panting desperately as I licked my lips. I noticed her glassy eyes staring directly into mine, lifeless but undeniably forgiving.

I screamed and recoiled away from her, falling into the shadows of Castle Dracula, pursued by horror and guilt of my own outer monster.

Wake up, White Rose! a voice screamed at me, seeming to jostle my very soul as one would throttle a body to wake them up from a deep sleep. My eyes shot open and I screamed as I sat up straight. I was in a large, dark room. Candles decorated the space, illuminating dressers and side tables, but only enough to reveal the boundaries of the room.

My scream echoed off the walls of my bedroom at Castle Dracula.

I pressed my fingers to my lips, frantically searching for fresh blood as I glanced left and right, checking for a person I might have been feasting on in my sleep. I saw nothing and felt no fresh blood on my lips. My heart raced wildly and I took great big breaths in an effort to regain my composure.

It had just been a dream. I hadn't really been hunting Claire.

It was guilt, a voice informed me, coming from within my own mind. *I felt it, too.*

I nodded stiffly, realizing that my hands were trembling. "I know, Envy," I whispered to my very real imaginary friend. I wore her black halo on my finger and we were now bonded as a result. I had first taken her halo when she'd been bonded with Leviathan, a fallen archangel, and she had shape-shifted to look like Claire. She had murdered Last Breath right before my eyes, and I'd killed her for it. I'd been under the impression that she'd also tortured and murdered Solomon, but I later discovered that Uriel had been behind that cruelty.

But she had proven her loyalty to me—as best as a former Sin could, at any rate. She'd been trying to rescue her lover, Azazel, one of the original watchers who conceived the first nephilim with human women.

Regardless, her actions had given me the terrible ultimatum of killing Claire or letting Envy escape unpunished. At the time, I hadn't known whether it really was Claire—being possessed by Envy—or if she was merely shapeshifting to mess with my head. I had killed her anyway, not wanting to risk letting the Sin escape.

And that visual would never leave my mind, which had been Envy's—Leviathan's—intent.

Now I was having nightmares about it, even though I had managed to save the real Claire from Greed's prison beneath A2C2—the rubble formally known as Abundant Angel Catholic Church. It had been destroyed in my battle with Greed and her pet wendigo. Now, the destroyed remains of the church were where the Conclave's Shepherds and nephilim army was camped.

Because, you know, everyone was at war. Heaven. Hell. Conclave. My misfit band of monsters.

Every party was seemingly against me and my people rather than each other. Even the Four Horsemen were more interested in arresting and prosecuting me than policing their own citizens: angels and demons.

Maybe my nightmare was specifically because I had saved Claire from Greed at the church. It had been days since I'd saved her and kicked off this new war, and she didn't seem to be getting any better at all. She slept fitfully, living in a reality of never-ending nightmares. She hadn't woken up yet.

I let out a frustrated breath, barely remembering coming to bed last night. Over the past few days, we had been engaged in guerrilla war tactics against any of the numerous enemies arrayed against my people. If we heard about a force on the move, we tried to shut them down. There was no open and clear battle line where everyone neatly lined up against each other and took turns lobbing sinful apples or spewing Latin prayers.

The war in Kansas City consisted of roving packs of ninjas, nephilim, vampires, werewolves, Shepherds, angels, demons, wizards, and any other Freak residing at Castle Dracula who wanted to join our hunting parties into the city proper.

The night that hundreds of blazing balls of fire had started falling from the sky, the Regulars had collectively shit themselves, declared a citywide emergency, and then they'd gotten the hell out of Dodge. Most of them.

Plenty still remained because this was America and rebellion was the backbone of our DNA, for better or worse. Those who had remained had hit the streets downtown with megaphones and *the End is nigh* posters draped over their backs and chests to preach salvation to the nonbelievers.

Their missionary endeavors had lasted one hour, tops. Because that was how quickly Alucard, Gunnar, and Ryuu's forces were on the streets to confront the threats.

They'd seen their first werewolf disemboweling a demon in front of their favorite Starbucks or an angel ripping a vampire in half by the bus stop and practically given themselves instant hernias in their haste to flee back to the safety of their homes or churches. The smart ones had fled town in a second wave of unrestrained panic. Most habitable buildings were now barred and padlocked as the last of the Regulars hunkered down in basements. We had encountered small groups of emergency services workers, but even they had seemed shell-shocked to see their first monsters hit the streets they were sworn to protect.

Exodus had come to Kansas City.

Revelations was yet to come.

Thankfully, Roland had teamed up with Samael and Alucard to put up their old crimson dome over the city to keep anyone from bringing reinforcements in. This time, they had discovered a way to leave me an exit strategy. As far as I knew, no one else could move in and out of the war zone without my permission.

Which was great, because the US military or National Guard would have had some really scathing critiques of Kansas City's new system of justice. We weren't big on juries or arrests. Our judges were here to hand out pocket constitutions and crack skulls, and they were all out of pocket constitutions.

I glanced over at Ryuu's side of the bed and noticed a folded piece of paper. I was annoyed to find him gone but a part of my heart warmed to find the little love note.

I opened it with a smile, ready to read his sweet little haiku or a litany of naughty suggestions for our upcoming day-date this afternoon.

"Scourge of demons at the plaza. Conclave acting shady. Horsemen scouting the city for you. Lay low for the day. Hope you like your new pillow. I stuffed it full of angel feathers. I'll pick you up at Xuanwu's for our date."

I frowned and crumpled up the paper. "Is it so much to ask for a little compliment or two?"

Envy chuckled in my mind. *The pillow was a nice touch. Like a cat leaving a dead mouse at the front door.*

I smiled and squeezed the pillow. It *was* really soft. I set it down, knowing I couldn't go back to sleep after my nightmare. I glanced down at my fingers and sighed, noticing the cuts and scratches marring my pale flesh from fighting angels and demons all day every day. I climbed out of bed and made my way to the shower.

It was so hard to get dried blood out from under the fingernails, and I had a big date today.

2

I made my way down the halls of Castle Dracula, idly taking note of the vampires and workers rushing to and fro as they delivered messages, reports, or requests from one part of the castle to another—from one group of warriors to another. I wore Aphrodite's white fighting gear since it couldn't get blood on it and it had the cool static cling ability where it could hold my weapons without the need for a sheath. It was also incredibly strong and durable.

And I looked great in it. I had a date today, damnit.

I also carried the small shoulder satchel—more like a flat messenger bag —that Last Breath had given me. It was bottomless, and that made me inordinately happy. The satchel would also be great if I happened to pick up any new haloes today. I didn't want to touch them directly unless I absolutely had to.

I turned left at the intersection and bumped into a big furry chest. I stepped back in a rush, instinctively gripping the hilt of my katana.

Kenai stared down at me. The giant kodiak grizzly looked about as amused as if I'd asked him if a bear shits in the woods. I poked him in the belly with my finger and made the requisite giggling sound. "Morning, Pillsbeary Doughboy," I drawled, emphasizing my modification to the phrase.

His lip curled back in a warning snarl, not finding my personalization humorous.

I lifted my hand to brush a loose strand of hair from my forehead and, in the process, I discreetly flashed him my bare wrist long enough for him to assess it. His eyes flicked down to verify the rune branded into my flesh but he made no indication that might be witnessed by a casual passerby.

The Omegabet had turned up a neat little rune for me—an anti-possession ward. No angels or demons could wear one—if they even knew about our application of it, which they didn't—so no one could secretly sneak around my castle pretending to be someone else. Like Leviathan had done with Claire.

Thankfully, it didn't prevent or disrupt my bond with Envy. Then again, I hadn't necessarily adopted her halo like Leviathan had. Technically, she was my prisoner. I had simply let her out on parole for good behavior with a figurative ankle bracelet that was a promise of eternal imprisonment inside Solomon's Prison. I also had handcuffs around her heart, which were even stronger. She wanted to save Azazel and Samzaya, the last of the watchers, and any attempt at betrayal would forever ruin her chance at reuniting with Azazel, her supposed lover.

As a rule, no one ever discussed the runes I had mandated everyone to receive. My people had swiftly and secretly scoured our ranks to verify that each warrior on my side was authentic rather than a shapeshifter, and then they had been taken to a private room to receive the small, almost unnoticeable brand. We had acted quickly and discreetly enough to get everyone branded before anyone had the chance to gossip about it—and we'd severely punished anyone caught openly discussing it, locking them away in solitary confinement with Tentacle Timmy.

I hadn't actually met Tentacle Timmy. Enough people had assured me that I never should and I had taken it as gospel. The mere implication that loose lips would earn you an extended sleepover with Tentacle Timmy had done wonders to silence practically everyone. I'd heard one story of a vampire who had accidentally mentioned the rune out loud and then he'd promptly leapt off the bridge to fall to his death rather than risk being sent to Tentacle Timmy's cell.

Long story short, everyone now had a rune that let the others know they were the real deal. Since no one spoke of them, the angels and demons didn't know of them. I knew it was only a matter of time before the simple tactic was outsmarted, but it helped us clarify who our allies really were.

SHAYNE SILVERS

It had only cost us seventy-three executions, which I'd been told was a good ratio.

We'd found seventy-three angels and demons attempting to pass as allies within Castle Dracula. They had all learned to avoid the Toymaker's security checkpoints to keep their true identities concealed, but my runes had caught them.

Kenai held out his massive paw as if he was telling me to halt, but in reality he was showing me the small rune branded into one of the pads of his paw. I didn't acknowledge Kenai's rune, and he lowered his paw as he glanced over my shoulder in a sweeping gaze, verifying that I was alone. Then he stepped to the side and gestured with his massive claw for me to pass.

"Great talk," I muttered.

He grumbled something back, but it wasn't remotely apologetic. I didn't blame him. I'd saved Claire and brought her back, but she wasn't even remotely the same woman he had loved a week ago. Claire was a broken, nightmare-plagued shell of her former self. And Kenai had been duped by the imposter Claire—Envy—in a manner that cut bone deep. He had supposedly slept with Leviathan-Envy, thinking she was the real Claire. I didn't know whether that was true or not and I didn't care to find out.

Leviathan had been a real bitch.

Do not absolve me of my part in those crimes, Envy murmured very softly in my mind.

I nodded. *I'm not. I'm also not going to rub your face in it. You can't forgive the past if you never forget the past. What's done is done, Envy.*

She did not reply, so I let it go as I made my way down the hall towards Claire's quarters. I rounded another corner and found half-a-dozen shifter bears guarding a single door. At the opposite end of the hall, I saw another bear standing guard to make sure that no one passed without the security rune.

The guards lifted their claws to wave at me, leaving their paws up a second longer than normal to show their runes, and then they lowered them to their sides. I did the hand brushing my hair back motion again, pausing to show them my wrist, before completing the gesture. Their eyes subtly took note of it but they gave no verbal acknowledgment.

Perfect.

I pointed my chin at the door. "Any change?" I asked.

10

They shook their heads and lowered their eyes. "No, White Rose," a black bear with a scarred face rumbled. One of his ears was torn as well, and I found myself wondering if it was from recent days or an older injury.

I sighed and made my way to the door. I slipped inside and softly closed it behind me. The room smelled of incense and lavender. I smiled crookedly and made my way into the dim interior. Claire's bed was backed up against the far wall, facing the door so that she would have a clear view of any guests the moment they entered. Of course, she hadn't woken up yet, so it wouldn't have mattered where I put the bed, but it made me feel better to consider these things for her. She slept fitfully, and I could see her eyes rapidly shifting beneath her eyelids. Her lips parted slightly and she let out a whisper of a whine that broke my heart. My knees buckled and I bit my lower lip. She had lost a lot of weight and her forehead was damp with sweat.

She looked like death.

"It's me, Claire," I whispered, blinking rapidly. "Callie."

I sensed no change to signify she had heard me or sensed my presence. Her hand peeked out from under her blanket; it was skeletal and pale. I masked my instinctive flash of panic upon not seeing the now-standard anti-possession rune on her wrist. Aala had been Claire's primary caretaker, and she had told me that the rune could very likely kill Claire in her current state. It wasn't very powerful or anything, but Claire was incredibly weak, and it did require a bit of magic from the person being branded—their inner Freak ability was the battery that initially powered it up and then kept it functioning.

It knocked humans flat out. We'd discovered that when my father had received his brand. He'd immediately passed out for twelve solid hours. He'd woken up with no recollection of the actual branding, so he'd related it to a spring break story where one woke up with a hangover, a new tattoo, and a few naked strangers passed out in the shared hotel room. Clearing your throat and calling out, "Mimosas?" was the only acceptable reaction to such situations.

He was currently working with Hephaestus in the forge since I'd determined it to be the safest place at the castle if he wanted to contribute. He'd refused to sleep at Solomon's Temple and lounge about at the library when there was 'manly work' to be done.

I think he was more afraid of Aphrodite's outrageous flirting. She took special pride in making my father uncomfortable, and he sought protection under the strict tutelage of his tormentress' husband, the Blacksmith God. My father was safe, so I didn't really care what he chose to do with his time.

I peeled my eyes away from Claire's bare wrist and swallowed my unease. Claire was not currently protected from possession, which was ironic since her current state was the *result* of her being possessed by Envy.

Then Greed and the wendigo had sunk their claws into her, torturing her in her prison cell beneath A2C2. No one knew what she'd been through down there, but she hadn't woken up since passing out in my arms—after accidentally touching Greed's halo and establishing a connection with the recently murdered Sin.

I'd banished Greed into Solomon's Prison, but not quickly enough to keep Claire safe from her. She couldn't reach her or torment her at the moment, but I wasn't sure what to make of the development. She seemed to be growing weaker and more frail by the day, and Aala had warned me that the lowest of demons could easily possess her in her current state. She was helpless. Was that why Claire hadn't woken up yet? Because I needed to let Greed fully bond with her? That wasn't going to fucking happen, of course. Turn her over to the very monster who had broken her? No way.

But...

Was *this* the alternative? To live within her own nightmares...forever, or until she wasted away to nothing?

Claire started muttering something in her sleep and I cocked my head as I tried to decipher it. "Dark...horse, d-dark h-horse..." she whispered in a panicked tone, her scratchy voice stuttering and stammering in an inconsistent cadence, as if I was only hearing part of her dreaded nightmare.

Hearing her speak at all made the hair on the back of my neck stand straight up, because this was the first time she'd made a cognizant statement. Her head rocked from side-to-side as if she was trying to get away from whatever she saw in her mind. It wasn't a violent motion that made me fear she was on the verge of a seizure, but more like she was in the throes of a fever dream. She quieted down and I realized I'd been holding my breath the entire time.

I let it out in a rush and quietly walked up to the bed to look down at her. I softly touched her wrist with my fingers as I bent over and kissed her on the forehead. "I'm so sorry, Claire," I whispered, fighting back a wave of guilt for not saving her sooner.

She suddenly lurched up and I jumped in alarm to see her eyes still closed. Before I could react, she wrapped her arms around my neck in a desperate hug, clutching onto me like I was a life preserver in a turbulent sea. "It hurts," she whisper-sobbed, trembling as she clutched me. "So. *Much!*"

Not knowing what else to do, I hugged her back just as tightly, blinking away my tears and trying to sound calm and reassuring rather than frantically ecstatic. "I'm right here, Claire. No one can get you. What hurts, honey?"

I felt her strength rapidly fading and I knew she was on the verge of collapsing back into unconsciousness. "Life," she whimpered. "*Life* hurts. Let me *die*," she pleaded, and then she fell limp, her arms sliding free of my neck.

3

I supported her dead weight and carefully settled her back down. Her eyes had remained closed the entire time, which made the skin on my forearms pebble. I gently tucked her back in under the covers and brushed a tear from her gaunt cheeks. I wasn't sure if she had truly woken up or if it had been part of her dream, but she had latched onto me and then answered a direct question. It hadn't been a coincidental statement from her dream. She had answered me specifically. That had to be progress.

"Goddamn you, Greed," I whispered, momentarily seeing red. "What the hell did you do to my best friend?"

Envy piped in with a sympathetic whisper. *I hate to tell you this...but your friend is worse than dead. She is untethered. There...is no bringing back the woman you remember. Her soul is completely ravaged. It's as bad as anything I've ever seen in Hell.*

I blinked, feeling my pulse spiking as I repeated the name of her tormentor, "Greed. Mammon," I added, deciding to throw in her angel name, even though I had already killed that part of the duo.

I can think of no one else capable of such viciousness, Envy whispered. *I am sorry, Callie.*

I pulled out Greed's halo—now a finger-sized ring of inky black thorns with red flecks—and clenched it in my fist. My entire arm was shaking and I was gritting my teeth. "I'm going to destroy it," I rasped as I stared at my battered friend.

Envy was silent for a few moments, but I could tell she had more to say and she was hesitant. *That would kill Claire directly. She is bonded to it now. In fact, it might be the only thing keeping her relatively aware at the moment. The shock of such a break in her current state might completely destroy her*, she said in a gentle tone.

I pointed at the room. "And this is so much better?" I hissed. "She asked me to let her *die!*"

The door to the room clicked closed and I spun to face the threat, extending my silver claws as I snarled protectively. Aala stared back at me with very wide eyes. She slowly lifted her hands to show me they were empty —and to reveal the rune branded on her wrist. "It's just me, Callie," she said in a careful tone.

I closed my eyes and took a calming breath as I retracted my silver claws and flashed her my own rune. "She spoke to me, Aala," I whispered, turning back to Claire. "She said she wants me to let her die. Then she passed back out. I don't even know if she actually woke up or if she was dreaming, but she answered a direct question."

Aala stepped up beside me and placed a comforting hand on my shoulder as she assessed her patient. "Well, that is a first. I have been unable to wake her yet. I'm sorry her first words were so unsettling."

I nodded numbly. "Wasn't exactly what I was hoping for," I said. "Envy tells me Claire's soul is ravaged and untethered. That there is no getting her back." I turned to look into Aala's eyes. "Is she right?"

Aala did not give me false hope, but she did not reassure me either. She walked up to Claire and rested the back of her hand on my friend's forehead with a thoughtful look on her face. Then she lowered her hand and turned to look at me. "There are pieces of Claire that are completely missing. There isn't a way for me to fix her chakras because parts of her soul are simply gone, like Envy says. What is left is not enough for me to sew back together, figuratively speaking. In time, there is a chance she could regrow those parts of her soul. Maybe..."

I nodded eagerly. "And? How long would it take for her to heal?"

Aala shook her head sadly. "I'm afraid Envy is correct. The Claire you knew is gone forever, Callie. Parts of her remain but they are no longer intact. To her, they may as well be memories. Dreams. And we are talking years and years to heal naturally from something like this. But...there has never *been* a patient who suffered something like this. Not that I've ever seen or heard of. Even if it was theoretically possible for a person to recover from this kind of trauma, I doubt Claire fits the parameters."

"Why?" I demanded. "She's a shifter! They heal from all sorts of injuries."

Aala frowned compassionately. "Because she has no reason to *want* to heal. She is living in a world of shattered dreams and torn memories that was once her real life. In addition, that mental landscape is now filled with just as many nightmares of her apparent torture and imprisonment—whatever she suffered as Greed's prisoner. She quite literally cannot tell which is real. She has no reason to want to heal because she has no memory of why she *should*. All she can remember is pain, torture, hatred, and violence. Greed did far, far worse than kill her. She let her *live*. I fear Greed drove her utterly mad."

I clenched my jaw and squeezed my fist, feeling like I could hear Greed's laughter echoing up from the ring in my hand. "Do what you can for her, Aala," I said in a hoarse tone. I stared down at Claire. "Fight this, Claire Stone," I demanded. There was no acknowledgment that she'd heard me as she stumbled through her eternal nightmarish dreamscape. I turned to leave the room.

I needed to destroy something.

Confronting Greed inside Solomon's Prison will only serve to embolden her, Envy chided in a no-nonsense tone. *It will accomplish nothing because she cannot be harmed there. You will be giving her a victory lap and you will gain nothing.*

What the hell am I supposed to do then, Envy? I demanded. *Let my best friend die? How about I just kill her myself?*

Envy let out a frustrated sound. *I could go visit her and try to get a read on the situation. Maybe play Uriel against her or complain about how you're abusing the agreement you made with me. Maybe Obie knows something that could help.*

I set my hand on the door and took a calming breath, hating that she was right. I'd trapped Uriel inside the Seal just to be certain he couldn't cause me any problems. I literally had no idea what to do with him. Knowing his soul or spirit or whatever remained of him was living large at the internal resort where Solomon's demons partied for eternity was not something that lifted my spirits. I wanted to send him down into the depths of Hell to pay for what he'd done.

But at least he couldn't cause me anymore grief.

Fine. I need answers, Envy.

With a thought, I sent her into the depths of the Seal of Solomon and figuratively crossed my fingers. I felt suddenly hollow without my bad conscience present, which was a very strange thing to admit.

I actually missed the devil on my shoulder.

4

I opened the door and stepped out into the hall. The guardian bears took one look at me and their ears hunkered low and their lips curled back in a wary snarl, anticipating danger of some kind from the look on my face. "Tell Cain and Roland to meet me on the balustrade. I'm going hunting," I commanded.

I didn't wait for a response as I stormed past them, gripping the hilt of my katana tightly enough for my knuckles to throb. I paused mid-step and felt the beginnings of a grim smile tickle my cheeks as I remembered something Aphrodite had obtained for me. I ripped open a Gateway to Solomon's Temple.

I stepped out onto the balcony and took a deep breath of the fresh, vibrant air of this sunny sanctum, which was the exact opposite of the perpetual night of Castle Dracula. Birds sang in the gardens below and the sun shone down on the temple, seeming to make it glow.

I briskly made my way to the entrance, scanning left and right as I entered the spacious halls in search of Aphrodite. I didn't hear or see anyone, so I made my way to her quarters, which wasn't very far from the entrance since she was now my Mistress of the temple, or whatever title she had changed it to today.

Aphrodite was a very...*grand* person—narcissists worshipped at her feet. She'd even managed to embellish her clothes, adding lace and silk to her garments in an effort to emphasize just how important she was. Since there were only a handful of people living here, and most of them were males who just wanted to ogle the three-dimensional pin-up doll, I was content to not find her strutting around in lingerie or leather dominatrix attire. I wouldn't have really cared if she had chosen to wear that, but it would have really killed Quentin and Adrian's research productivity.

The nephilim were innocent lambs when it came to encounters with the wolves of the fairer sex.

Then again, it might actually improve their productivity to do a little healthy ogling. I'd suggest it to Aphrodite. She'd love it. Like a spider with new flies, she was.

I finally reached Aphrodite's rooms and knocked on the rich, polished double doors. Then I pulled them open and entered, not bothering to announce myself because no one else would have dared walk into her chambers without permission.

"Morning!" I called out. "I'm here to pick up my new toys—" I cut off abruptly as Grace sauntered out of the bathroom. She wore a short silk robe that was obviously designed to be scandalous. I stared at the Easter Bunny, unable to make my mouth formulate words. She was petite yet curvy, and her soft white fur was damp from the shower. Her tall ears were decorated with silver hoop earrings, and she had a lot of tattoos that resembled the familiar geometric designs that kids painted on Easter eggs—except on her, they looked more tribalistic and primitive. They marked her ears, cheek, arms, and even her upper thighs—which had always been concealed to my eyes before this…strange moment in time. Dorian had told me that she got a new tattoo for every one-hundred confirmed kills.

Because the Easter Bunny was a notorious assassin. She also adored Faberge eggs, naturally.

Grace suddenly noticed my presence and let out a surprised squeak as she spun to stare at me with her huge, sapphire blue eyes. There was no white to speak of in her sclera. Just a field of blue with a black pupil in the center. Her surprise turned to confusion and then concern. "Shit," she said by way of introduction. "Was she off limits?" she asked me.

I stared back at the leggy, fluffy white bunny and I watched her ears twitch nervously.

Aphrodite strolled out of the bathroom in a matching silk robe that somehow looked more scandalous on her than it did on the Easter Bunny. Perhaps it was her curves.

Or maybe it was because she was the freaking goddess of sex.

Aphrodite walked up behind Grace and wrapped her arms around the Easter Bunny's waist. Grace's ears quivered with anxiety, even seeming to wilt as Aphrodite's hands slipped under her robe. I swear to God she subconsciously started thumping one of her feet and let out a full-body shudder at Aphrodite's touch.

The goddess of sex finally seemed to notice me standing in the open doorway, and she gave me a big bright smile. "Callie! You look stunning this morning!" she said with genuine cheer and absolutely zero shame.

I stared from one to the other in stunned disbelief. "What did you do?" I croaked.

Aphrodite gave me a confused frown and then glanced at Grace wrapped in her arms. Grace gave her no help, looking as if she wanted nothing more than to disappear. Aphrodite finally turned back to me with a perplexed look. "Well, I fucked the Easter Bunny, if that's what you're asking."

"Grace," the Easter Bunny clarified with a wince. "My name is *Grace*."

Aphrodite slipped her hands out from beneath Grace's robe and circled the fluffy white rabbit until they stood face-to-face. Aphrodite smiled predatorily and then kissed her right on the button nose. "Of course it is, my sweet."

I turned away from the pair, not wanting to witness a lover's spat this early in the morning. I saw a chest perched on the make-up table and I pointed at it. "Are those my new toys?" I asked.

"Oh, yes," Aphrodite purred. "Hephaestus just finished them for you. Take the whole chest. My dear husband says every weapon needs a sheathe. I look forward to the day when he recalls that his *wife* is a perfectly designed sheathe for his mighty hammer—"

"Got it!" I blurted, cutting her off as I made my way to the dresser and scooped the small ornate chest under my arm. "I'm going hunting if you aren't too busy, Grace," I said as I turned my back on them and made my way to the door.

"I'm coming!" Grace all but shouted.

Aphrodite burst out laughing. "It's like an echo of last night that just won't go away," she mused. Grace muttered a curse and began getting dressed.

"Meet me at Castle Dracula in ten minutes," I told her. She knew I would be leaving from the usual traveling spot, so it wasn't necessary to clarify. I escaped the furry Isle of Lesbos, but my mind raced with questions about the physical technicalities of their bizarre sextravaganza that were hammering my brain like a relentless hailstorm. I definitely needed to go distract myself by pulverizing some angels and demons.

5

Shadow Walked back to Castle Dracula and found Roland and Cain waiting for me. They showed me their wrists in a casual manner and I mirrored the now-familiar gesture. I made my way to the railing that overlooked Castle Dracula and started checking my weapons. The satchel was small enough to not get in my way while fighting, so that wasn't a concern. I shoved the golden box from Hephaestus inside and smiled to myself. Then I checked my silver katana at my hip, followed by the two pistols on my shoulder holster. I admired Aphrodite's white outfit and let out a sigh of relief.

I had two more new weapons at my disposal, but I didn't need to check on them. Thunder and Terror, the fiery swords from the Garden of Eden. Like the Spear of Destiny, they were sheathed within my soul and could be summoned into existence at a mere thought. I'd practiced doing just that repeatedly ever since I'd acquired them.

They were also a constant reminder of my parents, Constance and Titus, who had stolen the original fiery sword from Uriel in the first place. They hadn't wanted him using it to murder Azazel and Samzaya, so they'd taken it. Unfortunately, it had become part of them, consuming them as it split in two. They'd been hiding out in the Garden ever since they'd left me on the steps of Abundant Angel. In a bitter twist of fate, I'd finally found them, but I'd been unable to keep them in my life. Because the only way to give the swords to me had been for them to...well, shed their mortal coils.

They gave their lives away for me to have Thunder and Terror, and so I could become the new guardian of the Garden of Eden, whatever that entailed.

The swords were the only weapons capable of freeing Azazel and Samzaya. They were also the weapons Uriel had been prophesied to kill them with, but I'd ripped that page right out of the official timeline.

Did that mean prophecy in general was bunk, and that we could change it at any time? That free will was supreme, even when it came to dealing with angels and demons? Or possibly the Bible itself?

That sounded ominous and sanctimonious. Just because something could be changed didn't mean that it *should* be changed. I had no doubt that my actions would have unintended consequences. Whether that was for better or for worse was yet to be determined.

I'd traded in the Spear of Destiny to unlock the Garden of Eden and acquire the fiery swords, but...now what was I supposed to do? The only way to stop the nephilim threat was to go whoop the shit out of the watchers with my new fiery swords. We'd found their prison, but we hadn't been able to get inside of it yet. The two watchers were surrounded by an epic, definitely magical sandstorm. Lucky and the Four Divines were currently trying to break their way inside, but they had so far been unsuccessful.

Gunnar, Alucard, and Starlight were there in case the Divines succeeded prematurely and accidentally let the watchers loose on the world. Small chance, epic consequences.

That was another item on my to-do list for today. Without the nephilim on our side, Team Callie was going to suffer a loss when the final numbers were tallied. Convincing Azazel and Samzaya to help me was also the only way I could prove to everyone that the angels had kidnapped and brainwashed them for thousands of years. The nephilim were actually angel vampires or blood vampires, and I needed to release their dads from captivity to prove it—which was why Uriel had wanted to kill them. No evidence, no foul.

Revealing that would potentially turn the Vatican crew against Heaven, though it wouldn't do much for actually ending our fighting. Were we supposed to side with the demons? Was the Vatican supposed to side with me?

No one really knew what we were fighting for. Not that I'd heard. Gabriel and Wrath were obviously after something, but the rest of us were just running around with swords and guns, killing each other before anyone had a chance to lethally poke us. There were no such things as friends in fatal games of freeze tag.

I let out a frustrated sigh and turned to Roland. I had time to kill before my date with Ryuu, so this little hunting party would be a good workout, it would allow me to let off some steam, and it would give me a personal view of what was currently happening in the city. Maybe a goddamned clue as to why we were all at war in the first place.

That would be swell.

"Where can we go to kill some assholes and get a relatively safe look at the city?" I asked. "Preferably Horsemen free," I added, recalling at least *part* of Ryuu's warning note.

If he ever told me to stay home again, I was going to buy a tombstone with his name and the phrase *make me a sammich* on the front, and then I was going to leave it on his pillow as a surprise gift.

Roland shook his head and handed me an embossed card. I accepted it with a hesitant frown and read it, fearing Ryuu had left behind another note. Anger swiftly replaced my confusion. I pinched it between two fingers and lifted it to eye-level, fully intending to light it on fire.

Roland snatched it away and shook his head. "I don't like it either, Callie, but he does call a truce for the duration of the visit. This could be a peace offering, or he may have information we need. He wouldn't bother sending a card if it was a trap. That's not their style."

Cain cocked his head curiously. "What is it?"

I turned to him with a bitter smile. "Father Ignatius wants to have a private chat with me at my convenience."

Cain gripped his dagger instinctively and shook his head. "Fuck that guy. He was at the Dread Wedding."

Roland rolled his crimson eyes. "We were *all* at the Dread Wedding," he snapped, referring to the bloodiest nuptials I had ever attended—Samael and Lilith's wedding. "I'm not saying we should trust him, I'm saying we should hear what he has to say. It's called *gathering intelligence*. The invitation is from him—personally—not the Conclave. That is interesting because it is not official."

I let out a frustrated sigh, remembering the other things I needed to do today. If I didn't meet with Father Ignatius now, I didn't know when I would find the time. "Fine. Let's go hear him out, but if we sense anything fishy—"

"Heh-heh," Cain chuckled. "Catholics...fishy," he murmured, sounding like a Beavis and Butthead impersonation.

I ignored him and continued on. "If we get a bad feeling, we vamoose. If he makes me angry, we vamoose."

He nodded and pulled a glass marble from his pocket. "Even if his camp is warded, we can escape with these." I nodded and patted my satchel, letting him know I had one as well.

I turned to Cain. "Wait here and locate some assholes we can go fight when I return. We won't be long, and Grace should arrive in a few minutes to keep you company." He narrowed his eyes, obviously wanting to join me on my dangerous trip. "If things go badly, we're fleeing right back here and we could possibly have nephilim, Templars, and angry wizards chasing us down. Be ready to defend this balcony with extreme prejudice."

His eyes lit up at the suggestion of potential violence. "Fine. Don't take too long, Callie."

I leaned forward and kissed him on the forehead. "I love you too, Cain," I said.

He blushed and waved me off. "Get out of here." He backed up against the railing and folded his arms, resigned to wait and pout until Grace arrived. "Have fun at Bible Camp," he said with a smirk.

Roland held out a hand and I grasped it. Then he Shadow Walked us out of Castle Dracula.

✤ 6 ✤

We rematerialized outside the perimeter of what was left of Abundant Angel Catholic Church. It was surprisingly gloomy and dark outside, looking like heavy rain was on the way. It was so cloudy that the majority of the red dome covering the city was hard to detect. Thankfully, the dome didn't block rainfall, only living beings. If it did start raining, the warm air would make it tolerable.

Where the church had once stood was now a giant pile of rubble, broken furniture, and jagged sections of stone wall. Such a beautiful old structure had been reduced to what now looked like a cemetery of broken headstones.

The Conclave's camp was surrounded by a ward of glowing blue light that made me think of electric barbwire. It was at least twelve-feet-tall and stretched back the entire block. The Conclave had commandeered the whole street, including many of the buildings to use for sleeping quarters, kitchens, medical stations, and whatever else they needed. They had also set up a few of those giant emergency tents often found on mission trips overseas. I had no accurate count, but there had to be a few thousand men milling about within the security perimeter. Roland and I shared a long, meaningful look, and then we approached the entrance, which was guarded by two grim Shepherds who were on the young side. I held the invitation out in front of me so that they didn't panic and jump to the presumption that Roland and I had picked their establishment for a quick bite to eat.

I needn't have bothered. They immediately recognized us and motioned for us to approach.

"Please wait here, White Rose," one of the Shepherds said. "Father Ignatius is expecting you." His partner turned away and jogged into the camp to alert Father Ignatius of my arrival.

I arched a curious eyebrow at the remaining Shepherd. He looked to be a few years older than me, but he was definitely green compared to the Shepherds from my day as a SHIT. "And what does the rest of the Conclave think about him meeting me in private? Or the rest of the camp, for that matter?"

The Shepherd didn't bat an eye. "I don't believe Father Ignatius is very much concerned about what the rest of the Conclave thinks. Otherwise, he wouldn't be leading them."

I smirked and nodded. "Great to hear."

"I think Father Ignatius left his last fuck back somewhere on the road to Bethlehem a few decades ago," a new voice suggested.

The Shepherd on guard stiffened rather than chastising the voice for blaspheming. He didn't look pleased about his reaction, but he obviously recognized and feared the speaker.

Beckett Killian stepped out from behind a stack of crates and met my eyes. "Nice to see you again," he said.

Roland took a casually aggressive step closer, smiling hungrily at Beckett. I flung out my hand to stop his advance and he complied, although he did purse his lips in annoyance. "Beckett Killian. Traitor to your own people. Templar hack."

I noticed the Templar scarf hanging down his chest like a bandana and I gave Roland a meaningful look. Those scarves blocked pretty much all magic, so a fight would resort to guns, fangs, and claws. On that note...

"Why aren't you in your vicious little sunbear form?" I asked sweetly.

Roland snorted. "Probably because no one would take him seriously any longer. I'm more frightened of a honey badger than a cuddly sunbear."

Beckett grinned from ear-to-ear rather than taking offense. It was actually unsettling to see how calm he was in the face of our mockery. "You got me," he said, flashing his teeth. Then he glanced over his shoulder and nodded. "Looks like Father Ignatius is on his way," he said, turning back to me with an intense look that bordered on psychopathic. "I really can't wait to catch up with you, Callie. Soon." He pointed a finger over my shoulder.

"Out there, doll." Then he winked and turned away, strolling back into the camp without a care in the world.

I glared at his back, clenching my fists. "On a scale of one-to-ten, how offended would you be if I ripped his spine in half right now, Shepherd?" I asked without looking at him. "How much would it cost me to bribe you to look away for three seconds?" Beckett slipped out of view and I muttered a curse before turning back to the Shepherd with a scowl. "Blew your chance, pal."

The Shepherd on guard let out a slight breath and pursed his lips. "The Templars are dangerous," he said, meeting Roland's eyes. "Be careful of provoking them, from one Shepherd to another," he said. "Things are different these days...Shepherd Haviar." I blinked in surprise to hear this young buck showing Roland some respect even though Roland had been ex-communicated after becoming a vampire.

I peered past the guard to see Father Ignatius speaking with a man in a hooded jacket, jeans and white sneakers. He had shaggy blonde hair and he didn't seem cowed by the head of the Conclave. He wasn't dressed like any of the Shepherds or Templars either. He was dressed like...a Regular.

The two ended their conversation, and the hooded young man simply walked away rather than bowing or groveling or making the sign of the Cross. Interesting.

Father Ignatius made his way out of the camp and walked right up to me with a polite smile. He was a frail old man with wispy white hair, and his robes hung from his shoulders like a wet shirt on a hanger. His eyes were the familiar milky white of all Conclave members, but he had a kind face. Determined, but kind. "Ah, White Rose. I am so glad you accepted my invitation to chat."

I nodded, taken aback by his bravery. He was closer to me than his own Shepherd, and he was no longer within the safety of his camp. "Curiosity killed that cat," I said, trying to read his body language for some hint as to why we were here and why he seemed so casually dismissive of the danger I represented to him. "Who was the Regular?" I asked, pointing at where I had last seen the hooded man.

Father Ignatius gave me a perplexed frown and then turned to look where I pointed. "Oh," he said, turning back to me with a dismissive wave of his hand. "A messenger with news from back home. He didn't even bring me any wine, the cheapskate."

The Shepherd on guard chuckled softly, but Father Ignatius didn't seem to run a very tight ship, because he didn't chastise the Shepherd for his lack of professionalism.

He turned to Roland and bowed his head slightly. "Roland Haviar," he said in a surprisingly reverent tone. "You are practically a legend here, even after all that has happened in recent years." The Shepherd on guard nodded his agreement and I flashed Roland a smile. "It is an honor to meet you."

Roland was polite enough not to bring up the Dread Wedding, but it was obvious that we *all* remembered it vividly and that we collectively agreed to pretend the insane bloodbath had never happened—like the majority of family gatherings, really. "I am pleased to make your acquaintance, Father Ignatius Rayebolera," Roland said in a respectful tone, although he did make sure that his fangs were just barely poking out from beneath his lips for all to see.

Father Ignatius lifted a finger to his own canines and grinned at Roland, startling my old mentor with his directness. Then the old man turned to me and I had to force myself not to flinch back from his intense, milky white gaze, since I couldn't quite tell where he was specifically looking. "Can you agree to a truce for the duration of this conversation?" I nodded and murmured my agreement, as did Roland. "Excellent. I call a truce as well. Now, child, would you prefer to walk or sit?" he asked me, "and out here or in my camp?" he added, pointing at both options.

I frowned, taken aback that he was willing to walk around with me beyond the safety of his camp. "I...let's walk out here," I finally said. "I haven't been back to the church since...well, the night we first met."

Father Ignatius nodded sadly and then he simply walked up beside me and hooked his spindly elbow within mine. I shot Roland a baffled look and I noticed the Shepherd on guard was grinning his amusement. Then we were walking, and I decided to start paying attention to my feet as Father Ignatius led me towards the destroyed church.

After a dozen paces of silence, I finally let out a frustrated breath. "Okay, Father Ignatius. What is this all about?" I asked in a stern yet polite tone. "What game are we playing, because I have a lot on my plate right now, and I'm sure you do as well."

"Direct. I prefer that." He took a deep breath and then detached himself from my arm. He took a few steps and then pointed at the rubble. "I wanted to discuss this in person rather than via a letter or messenger," he said in a saddened tone. "I believe we found the remains of Greta and Father David," he said in a somber tone.

❦ 7 ❦

I closed my eyes for a moment and then let out a calming breath. "Damn it," I whispered. "Are you sure it was them?" I asked, not even caring that I sounded desperate.

Father Ignatius gave me a compassionate look. "Father David is the man who found you on the steps, from what I hear." I nodded. Father Ignatius murmured a prayer for them, but I didn't have the heart to join in as I stared at the destroyed church. I had done this. Good intentions didn't count. "To be transparent, our best guess is all we can provide. The damage to their bodies..." he trailed off with a grim look. "To the best of our knowledge, the bodies we found belong to Father David and Greta. My condolences."

I nodded. "I never liked Greta, but I wouldn't have wished this upon anyone."

He nodded. "If we find further confirmation, I shall let you know." He turned to study the church, giving me a few moments of privacy to collect myself. I wiped at my eyes and patted my cheeks, promising to mourn later. It would do me no good here and now.

I walked up beside him and shook my head as I surveyed the chaotic scene. "Such a waste," I said.

He murmured his agreement and we stood in silence for a few more moments. Then he turned to look at me with a thoughtful frown. "I'm surprised you were willing to meet with me out in the open. The Horsemen are still looking for you, from what I hear."

I nodded with a grimace. "They're persistent like that," I grumbled. I looked over at him with a suspicious frown. "Why are you being so cordial. We're at war."

He surveyed his camp with a grandfatherly gaze, looking protective. "Are we? I must admit that it feels more like policing than warring."

I folded my arms. "Then why don't you go back home and let us sort it out? Better yet, let Heaven and Hell sort it out themselves, far away from here."

He smiled sadly. "Could *you* walk away?"

I lifted a finger. "I actually cannot walk away because this *is* my home. They invaded, not me."

He looked at me with very wise, sage-like eyes. "And did you not do something to warrant this scrutiny? Whether intentional or not is irrelevant. I make no accusations. I'm just an old man who likes to ramble on and ask difficult questions."

I grunted, realizing I kind of appreciated his candor. For an enemy, at least. "If you're feeling so chatty, how about you tell me who gave you the black bracelets for your nephilim?"

His happy demeanor shut down like a falling guillotine and he sighed. "Ah. That, I cannot do, White Rose. I keep my vows."

I took a calming breath, convincing myself not to kidnap or murder him right here and now. He was very strong yet he was all alone. Killing him would eliminate one of my larger problems—the nephilim. But...it didn't seem honorable. We were here under parlay.

"Why don't you call off your men, at least," I suggested. "Keep an eye out on the rest of us while we fight each other to death. That way you can keep your hands clean and your honor intact."

He smiled mischievously. "Why didn't you say what you truly thought? That I could ultimately send my men in after the battle to take out the weakened victors when they least suspect it?"

I studied him pensively. "You're not as nice as you let on, are you, Padre?" I asked with a faint smile.

Rather than laughing it off, he gave my question considerable thought. "I am a *strong* man," he finally said, choosing his answer very intently.

I frowned curiously. His words tickled something in my memory. Then it hit me, although I couldn't remember where I'd heard it. "Weak men make hard times. Hard times make strong men. Strong men make good times. Good times make weak men," I said, watching him closely.

His eyebrows almost jumped off his forehead as he stared at me. "That is *precisely* the power I was referencing. G. Michael Hopf was incredibly wise to pen those words. Do you read poetry?"

I grimaced and shook my head. "Not unless gangster rap counts. I think I saw it on a poster." Father Ignatius looked momentarily crestfallen to realize that I was not the poet he was hoping for.

He waved a hand. "No matter. You read more of Michael Hopf and I will listen to some gangster rap. A fair trade," he said, and then he extended his hand for us to shake on it.

I burst out laughing and then shook his hand. "Why not?" I said, still chuckling.

He grinned toothily and then motioned for me to walk with him. "May I speak freely, Miss Penrose?" he asked after a time. I turned to look at him and then gave him a slow nod. "Good. I do not believe they are here for you, specifically."

I snorted dubiously, wondering why he'd wanted secrecy. Maybe that was also why he'd suggested a walk outside of his camp. Did he suspect spies in his midst? "The Horsemen sure are," I finally said.

He nodded, but it was hesitant and placating. "True. But they came *after* your troubles started." He stared out at the distant skyline and shook his head, seeming mildly troubled. I realized he was scanning the sky for angels or Horsemen and I felt a shudder roll down my spine. The man was paranoid. "There is something they are not telling us. I'm here specifically to serve Heaven, and they won't even come clean with *me*, but I can sense it." He let out a mirthless chuckle. "Perhaps I'm just a nosy old man who believes I have the right to know important things. Far be it from me to dare question an angel, let alone an archangel."

I nodded my agreement to his paranoia, not his defensive dismissal. "I get the same feeling," I murmured. I didn't mention Wrath's wedding proposal, which definitely had something to do with their arrival, because I didn't want to give Father Ignatius another reason to fear me or paint me with the scarlet letter by association. "I think we are pawns in something much bigger than a fight for Kansas City. I think this is Angel War 2, and we're just an expendable land mass for them to utilize as a battlefield."

He nodded but did not comment.

"What brings you these suspicions?" I asked. "Your messenger?" I teased.

He frowned and gave me a confused look. Then it clicked and he let out a snort. "Oh, Aiden. That man isn't even Catholic," he muttered disgustedly. "The wandering angels were a pretty clear sign that something was definitely wrong. Especially when I saw them attack fellow angels," he said, bringing us back on topic.

"Well," I began, drawing out the word, "we did see them fall from the sky. Maybe they aren't truly angels anymore."

Ignatius nodded absently, although he didn't seem persuaded by my suggestion. "Perhaps, but why not openly say as much, if that is the case?" he asked rhetorically.

He glanced over my shoulder and frowned. Three nephilim were patrolling the street beyond the camp, putting them less than a dozen paces away from me and I hadn't even noticed. They were staring at me with violence in their eyes. Father Ignatius snapped a finger and the three nephilim collapsed in unison, looking like their legs had been swept out from under them. I arched an eyebrow, appreciating Father Ignatius' level of precision. I'd felt only a whisper of magic from him, so he was obviously attempting to conceal his true potential from me. Masking your true power level was a typical wizard move.

I was doing it right now as well, so I couldn't judge him for it.

He pointed a gnarled finger at the three nephilim. "We are under truce!" he scolded. As they were climbing back to their feet with chagrined faces, I took a moment to study their black bracelets more closely. They almost looked to be made of a shiny fabric of some kind.

I considered Shadow Walking up to one of the nephilim and kidnapping him, but then they were hurriedly walking away. Father Ignatius was staring at me, and I hadn't even noticed it since I'd been practically licking my lips at the thought of abducting a nephilim.

"Please do not do anything foolish, White Rose," he said, almost as if he had read my mind. "You've been doing so well thus far."

8

I narrowed my eyes and folded my arms. "Was I that obvious?" I asked with a somewhat abashed smile, hoping to ease his concern.

He continued staring at me. "I am quite familiar with manipulation tactics. Judging genuine personas from fraudulent, and reading body language, for example," he said, almost looking amused.

I narrowed my eyes. "What, were you a spy in your previous life?"

He chuckled. "Everyone at the Vatican is a spy," he admitted with a conspiratorial grin.

"I see why they put you in charge of the Conclave," I admitted.

"I'm glad you approve."

I snorted. "I didn't say I approved, I said I understand *why* they did it. As a general rule, I don't approve of my adversaries being more savvy than I originally assumed. It makes me twitchy."

He grinned and bowed his head. "And you, White Rose, are not quite the heathen I was led to believe."

"I'm still Master Dracula," I reminded him. "Although not by choice, for what it's worth."

He furrowed his brow curiously. "That is a story I would like to hear."

"Sure. Right after you tell your men to stop attacking my men. Or you can wrap up one of your nephilim and gift him to me as a peace offering."

His amusement faded rather quickly and he shrugged his shoulders as he turned us around and guided us back towards his camp, signaling that we were nearing the end of our bizarre exchange. "The nephilim might be under my care, but they do not seem to be under my supervision," he said very carefully. "It would be more accurate to say they tolerate my commands... when they don't conflict with their other commands." He gave me a small, knowing nod. "You said something about us being pawns before," he said, by way of explanation. "I tend to agree."

I let out a frustrated sigh, admitting to myself that if not for the archangels and sins, Father Ignatius may have been able to mend the bridge between my past discretions and the Vatican. Go figure.

"Well, if you could dampen their passion a little bit, I would greatly appreciate it. I really don't want to kill any nephilim. We share the same blood, after all."

Father Ignatius assessed me with a thoughtful gaze and then gave me the briefest of discreet nods. "I will try, but heed my earlier warning. I am not truly their master. I cannot sell you a vehicle that I am only leasing."

I nodded. "Better than nothing, Father Ignatius..." I trailed off awkwardly, forgetting his last name.

He smiled in amusement, his eyes seeming to twinkle. "Rayebolera," he offered. "No offense taken." His smile stretched even wider and he leaned closer to whisper conspiratorially. "I rather prefer your earlier moniker, Padre," he admitted with a guilty smile.

I laughed at his boyish mirth and shook my head. "I can live with that. Call me Callie."

His responding smile was much warmer this time. "Callie is much better than Master Dracula."

I nodded. "It never seemed to truly fit. I just picked it up along the way," I admitted with a shrug.

"Such is life. We pick up bags and carry them forward for years, never stopping to ask ourselves why we picked them up in the first place or why we still carry them with us."

"Don't tell me you write fortune cookies," I teased. "No. Wait. That's John 3:16, isn't it?"

He groaned and dramatically clutched at his chest as if I'd mortally wounded him. "Oh, the shame!" he rasped, grinning like a playful grandfather. "Now I see why you never quite fit in with the Conclave."

I took it as a compliment. "Preposterous! I've always had a thing for crotchety old men who scowl all the time," I said, licking my lips hungrily. "Yum."

He made the sign of the Cross over his chest and murmured a prayer. "She knows not what she does, Father."

I rolled my eyes. "What baggage do you carry these days, Padre? Seems like your new job would have a lot of it," I said, eyeing a pair of nephilim walking towards us from the camp. They kept their distance but they watched me in their peripheral vision, definitely wary of my presence, let alone my close proximity to Father Ignatius, who had no protective detail in sight.

He shrugged. "I'm an old man, so I have learned to drop my bags." He let out a polite laugh. "Or get someone else to carry them for me," he added.

I spotted Roland still standing at the entrance of the camp. He tracked me with his eyes, not seeming to breathe. A few Shepherds walked past him with a friendly wave. He didn't acknowledge their presence in the slightest, keeping his gaze fixed firmly on me.

"Well, Padre, I should get going before Roland turns into stone."

Father Ignatius turned to look at Roland and grew silent. "He has quite the reputation among the Shepherds," he said in a respectful tone.

I smiled proudly. "Yeah. He's a strong man, too. Like you and your poet."

"The most dangerous ones usually are," he said with a smile. His tone told me it was a compliment, even though the words could have been taken multiple ways. A warning, for example.

I wasn't too concerned if it was. "Well, I hope we don't meet across the battlefield. I'll do my best to avoid it, but I won't run from it," I told him.

"Agreed," he said with a resigned sigh. "I will add you to my prayers, Callie."

"Thanks, Padre," I said. Then I extended my hand. He studied it for a moment and then reached out to give me a firm shake. His hand was brittle and leather-skinned, but his grip was very strong.

He escorted me back to Roland, dipped his chin respectfully at the ex-Shepherd, and then he strode back into his camp, dipping his chin at the Shepherds on guard duty. Roland watched him like a hawk until he was out of sight. Then he grabbed my hand and tugged me away from the camp so that we were walking back down the sidewalk in front of the church, retracing my journey with Father Ignatius.

"What did you learn?" he asked.

It finally started to rain, but not very hard. As I'd thought, it felt refreshing rather than depressing. I told Roland everything I had discussed with Father Ignatius, leaving nothing out. He murmured a soft prayer upon hearing about Greta and Father David—mostly Father David, because Greta was horrible—but he was silent for the rest of my debrief. When I was finished, we continued on in silence for a few moments as he processed it all.

I cleared my throat and he glanced over at me. "Remember that messenger I pointed out?" I asked. Roland nodded. "Notice anything strange about him?"

Roland considered my question and finally shook his head. "I didn't get a good look at him, and he was too far away to smell. You said he was a Regular."

I nodded. "I *said* that," I agreed, "but I didn't *believe* it."

Roland frowned. "What?"

"Padre said the messenger brought him news from back home." I arched an eyebrow at Roland. "Strange, seeing as how there is a giant red dome blocking people from coming and going. My path is the only way in or out, and it's a big fat secret."

Roland looked suddenly troubled. "He lied to you."

I nodded. "Don't get all bent out of shape about it. Liars are more predictable than most people. You know what drives them so it's easier to anticipate their moves. Padre also hinted that he's not truly in charge of everything at camp, and Beckett sure seemed awfully confident of himself. Maybe Father Ignatius *wanted* me to notice his obvious lie. Like a secret message."

Roland looked even more concerned. "What in the world would the head of the Conclave need you to save him from?"

I grunted. "Probably something super awesome that I will absolutely hate saving him from," I said drily. "Anyway, the messenger's name is Aiden. Sounds like the name of a guy who cries after sex, so I doubt he's who Padre was concerned about. But at least we have a name to start looking into."

Roland cringed at my analysis and shook his head in disapproval. "Let's get back to Castle Dracula. Cain's probably worried sick about his sister."

I rolled my eyes and Shadow Walked us back to Castle Dracula.

9

ain and Grace were bickering back and forth when we arrived. Grace wore her leather vest and pants, sporting about twenty sheathed throwing knives. Two curved daggers hung at her hips, easily as long as her forearm. Grace turned to glare at me and flung her paws up into the air. "You said ten minutes!" she complained testily, even as she flashed me her anti-possession rune. I mimicked the gesture as Cain and Roland did the same. An ounce of prevention was worth a pound of cure, as they said.

Cain frowned at Grace and then shot me a questioning look, obviously confused by her tone.

I grinned. "I interrupted her earlier."

"From sleep?" Cain asked with a frown. "That's called morning. Happens every day."

I laughed and shook my head. "I caught her being naughty," I said, grinning at her. "You should take lessons from her, Cain. You might learn a thing or two."

Grace's foot started thumping into the ground and she folded her arms defiantly. Cain waited impatiently, his eyes darting from me to Grace with growing interest. "Oh? Do tell," he begged greedily.

In the same tone as a town crier reading a royal decree sent down to the masses from the castle on the hill, I cleared my throat and cupped my hands around the sides of my mouth like I was speaking to a crowd. "Hear ye, hear ye! The Easter Bunny fucked Aphrodite," I announced.

Cain's jaw dropped and he sputtered incredulously. Then he wrapped his arms around Grace and picked her up, spinning her around in a circle as he laughed joyously. "YAY!" he squealed. "I need details! Please!"

Grace scowled at me over his shoulder as she twirled around and around. "Thank you, Callie. Truly," she said drily.

I winked. "No problem."

"If I promise to spill the details, will you let me down?" Grace demanded as she thumped Cain on the head with the hilt of a dagger.

His deliriously happy smile reminded me of a kid at Christmas. "Oh yeah!" he cheered as he set her down and gave her an unrequested high-five.

Roland cocked his head and stared at Grace with a baffled expression, obviously giving it some deeper thought than Cain's caveman brain. Whether it was curiosity or confusion poking his brain, it was delightful to observe.

"Okay. Let's finally go on that hunt," I said in a loud voice, silencing Cain. "What did you find for me?"

He nodded studiously and pulled out his phone. He scratched his stubbled chin with a thoughtful frown as he scrolled down with his thumb for a few moments. "Got it. Ryuu is down near the plaza with some vamps and ninjas, fighting demons and Templars. I think there were one or two Shepherds in their mix, so he has his hands full. Then our favorite psychos, the wandering angels, stumbled into the fray and started killing everyone within reach, turning it into a real shit-show."

I growled angrily upon mention of the wandering angels—the term everyone was using to describe the fiery comets we had seen falling from the sky days ago. It turned out that they actually had been angels at one point, and something had sent them crashing down to Earth in a frenzy. Unfortunately—for absolutely everyone—the angels were stark-raving mad. Even Father Ignatius had said something similar about them. They were mindless, screaming, preaching zealots who would kill a fellow angel as often as a demon. No one knew why they had fled Heaven, why they had come here, or what had pushed them over the edge.

It was troubling, to say the least. All parties had universally—though unofficially—declared them enemies. No matter which side of the fight you were on, slaughtering wandering angels was part of your job.

But some of them were very adept at fighting, so it wasn't a simple or easy task.

Roland held up a finger. "Ryuu was very clear that the Horsemen are actively searching for you and that you needed to keep a relatively low profile, so heading directly to the frontlines would not be wise. Ryuu would be upset, the nephilim would go berserk to see the object of their hatred personally show up—which would rally their cause—and you may very well inadvertently bring the Four Horsemen down upon your own allies."

I narrowed my eyes at him, hating that he was right. "Has anyone said how amazing it is that the Four Horsemen are so incredibly helpful at, I don't know, maybe helping *everyone* by taking out the wandering angels themselves? Instead of hunting me, for example." Roland pursed his lips in agreement but gave me an exaggerated shrug as if to say, *it is what it is.* "Fine. Anywhere else?"

Cain cleared his throat and glanced back down at his phone to read from his encrypted messenger app. "A few vampires are talking about an orphanage that was overrun by demons. Apparently, they still have kids inside."

Roland snarled. Kids in danger always dialed his fury up to an eleven. "Where? And how long ago?"

Cain rattled off an intersection near the orphanage. "One hour ago," he added, reading the timestamp.

I nodded eagerly. "Then the kids might still be alive!"

Roland tore open a Gateway of crimson sparks and lifted his foot to step through to the intersection Cain had given him. "Let's get to work," he said in a gravelly tone.

I stepped through the Gateway after Roland. "Finally."

✺ 10 ✺

The wandering angel choked and gagged on her own blood mere inches away from my smiling face.

Some of that blood spattered my cheeks and mouth—enough for it to drip from my chin, although the rain was already working to wash it away.

"Father David taught me to never turn down a free warm meal," I whispered with a smile as I stared deep into the wandering angel's eyes and licked my lips.

Upon contact, my tongue buzzed with electrical energy and my gums tingled as my fangs extended. My eyes threatened to roll back into my head and I shuddered at the immediate rush of energy. But I composed myself... like a fucking lady.

I stared into the abyss of those crazed, soulless, surprisingly startled eyes and smiled triumphantly as I watched the life slowly fade away. "Hey, Cain?" I murmured, cocking my head curiously. "She looks surprised. That's the first relatively human emotion I've seen from one of them."

"Don't give a fuck," he replied, sounding bored and slightly out of breath. "They're assholes. Deranged murdering assholes," he grumbled as he violently yanked his dagger from the chest cavity of another wandering angel. "I'd be surprised to find two fiery swords suddenly buried in my ribcage too."

I smirked. "Yeah." Although the fiery swords were ablaze from hilt to tip, they did not burn my hands. They were a part of me. I swiveled my wandering angel so that her back was facing Cain. "Hey. Are the tips of the swords still on fire?"

"Yep," he said. "Totally disgusting, by the way. Like an angel kabob."

"So cool," I murmured. I saw Grace and Roland fighting further down the street, but they were helping a few groups of vampires and werewolves, so I couldn't see who they were fighting. Demons? More wandering angels?

"We should really get you off the streets, Callie," Cain added in a protective tone. "What if one of the four whores' sons show up?"

I rolled my eyes. "The Horsemen won't find me. I've only been out in the open for five minutes." I purposely chose not to count my time with Father Ignatius earlier.

He grunted. "How quickly can they appear again? Something like a bolt of lightning, right?" he asked sarcastically. I let out a weary sigh and risked a quick glance up at the sky in search of my hunters. Cain wasn't wrong. I'd been keeping a very low profile, only showing up for brief violent encounters or skirmishes where my people needed help before I changed battlefields or fled back to shelter at Castle Dracula.

If not for the Toymaker's newly made Guardians, even Castle Dracula wouldn't have been able to keep the Horsemen away. I needed to do something to get them off my back, but they refused to hear me out. I was apparently guilty no matter what the circumstances were. I let out an annoyed sigh and focused back on the task at hand.

The wandering angel's desperate hold on my forearms grew weaker until she slowly slid free of my fiery swords and collapsed to her knees before me. Then she toppled to her side with a final death rattle, splashing into a puddle before growing completely still. The wounds in her stomach were charred at the edges.

Well done.

The fire from my swords coughed and sizzled as the rain started falling harder and louder. I slowly shifted my attention to the remaining wandering angel, who was standing in the middle of the street and staring at me with a blank expression. He hadn't come to help his siblings against me and Cain. He'd just watched us, as if patiently waiting his turn. His once-elegant white robes were now stained with soot and practically threadbare in places. His long hair was greasy and matted and his scarred face was rough and unwashed. Even through the filth and neglect, I knew he had once been gloriously beautiful.

No longer. His unexpected fall from Heaven—or whatever the hell had really happened after I became the new guardian of the Garden of Eden—had shaken him. These angels were essentially refugees. Crazed, zealous, panicked refugees. They plagued the city and hunted anyone with even a sliver of supernatural ability—demon, fellow angels, werewolves, wizards, Shepherds, or vampires. They had been cast down into a world of strange, scary monsters and everyone was an enemy.

Half of them were unable to even articulate their rage or fear, so they lashed out at anything with even a glimmer of power in their blood. I'd tried reasoning with them the first few times I'd encountered one over the last couple days, and I had quickly learned that they were incredibly dangerous and that attempting to communicate with them was a great way to get murdered mid-greeting.

So, we'd just started exterminating the wandering angels before they could exterminate more of us.

The surviving wandering angel snarled at me like a caged beast and then he rushed me. I watched him approach with a calm, austere look on my face as the storm above us raged. At the last moment, I pirouetted and lashed out with my swords. Thunder and Terror tore through the crazed wandering angel, cutting him entirely in half.

He gasped as the two halves of his body collapsed to the ground beside his recently murdered partner. He stared up at me, his mouth opening and closing like a fish on dry land.

"You should have just walked away when I told you to," I muttered with a grimace. I let my blades wink out of existence and met his eyes. "We're supposed to be on the same side. I can't help you if you won't tell me what happened—"

My words cut off as I realized that his open eyes were already lifeless. I watched raindrops splash into them with zero reaction from the dead angel. I let out an annoyed sigh and turned back to the archaic building in the near distance. Sacred Heart Orphanage. I noticed a flurry of activity around the exterior of the building but no one seemed eager to go inside. Grace and Roland were now pushing down a side street, chasing their enemies further from the orphanage.

"I'm going to go check on the rabbit and the pastor," Cain told me before taking off into an easy jog.

I absently checked the pockets of the wandering angels, wondering if they might have some information that might help me determine what they were doing here, how they had fallen, or maybe a flyer's license with a name and an address on it. Maybe a job title: *Angel Mop-really-well, janitor at Pearly Gates*.

I'd read up on the angel hierarchy and it consisted of three spheres.

The First Sphere was the highest level and included the Seraphim, the Cherubim, and the Thrones.

The Second Sphere included the Dominions, the Virtues, and the Powers.

The Third Sphere was the lowest level and included Principalities, Archangels, and angels. Which was confusing, because everyone assumed archangels were the top of the totem pole. Envy had tried explaining it to me but Eae had repeatedly contradicted her claims. Eae had been involved with the angels much more recently than Envy, but he was also significantly lower in rank—the Third Sphere.

Basically, their structure was as dysfunctional as everything else I had seen firsthand from Heaven and Hell, and the academic credibility of my research materials was suspect—obtuse online forums or Wikipedia—so I wasn't too confident I had the grounds to argue with anyone either.

I found nothing helpful on the dead angels. Not even an angel blade. The Winchesters were fucking liars.

I rose to my feet and relaxed my shoulders. I stood in the center of the gloomy street and stared up at the gothic castle a block away. Rain hammered down from the pregnant black clouds and ominous thunder rumbled in an unceasing growl that seemed to shake the pavement at times. My hood was up to keep my hair relatively dry while I let the heavy rain wash all the blood from my hands and clothes.

I finally let my eyes settle on the dead bodies lining the street and I clenched my jaw before kicking the first dead wandering angel in the jaw hard enough to snap her neck. Not all the werewolves and ninjas had died, but there were enough of them to tally up this encounter as a stunning defeat. If we'd gotten here sooner, we might have saved some lives. The survivors were helping each other with smelling salts, bandaging wounds, and dragging their bodies to the shelter of a nearby shop's overhang. I strode down the center of the street and dipped my chin at my allies. They cheered determinedly at my swift defeat of the seriously lethal wandering angels who had caught them off-guard.

I frowned. Even three angels shouldn't have been able to run roughshod over this many wolves and ninjas. The majority of my allies seemed to be gathering outside the orphanage, so I pressed onward. Soon, I saw more dead bodies, but these belonged to demons as well as my allies. That explained it.

The wandering angels had stumbled onto my allies after or during their battle with these demons, attacking them from behind. Same tactic as Ryuu was facing a few blocks away, according to Cain's messenger app. Coincidence? Maybe the wandering angels were just attracted to the magical auras of so many Freaks, angels, and demons fighting, like vultures and crows to a battlefield, or a shark sensing blood in the water from a mile away.

Or flies to dog crap.

"Fucking wandering angels. They're like drunken, feral rats," I muttered to no one in particular, even though several of my allies flinched at my sudden outburst.

Were Gabriel and Wrath behind their arrival? Or maybe it was my fault for taking over the Garden.

I let out a frustrated breath and made my way to the huddle of vampires and werewolves outside the entrance to the orphanage. "You guys okay?" I asked. They nodded and murmured in the affirmative, but many cast wary, concerned glances at the entrance to the orphanage. "How many did you send inside?"

A naked woman walked up to me, subtly letting me know she was either a werewolf or a nudist. "The werewolves could get in but we couldn't shift once inside. A few ninjas could enter but their swords were utterly ineffective against the demons' armor," she said, pointing at two dead bodies in black garb on the sidewalk. "Vampires were equally unsuccessful, and then we were attacked out here."

I scowled up at the orphanage with a frown, wondering what kind of ward could cause so many problems and how a group of demons could have gotten their hands on it.

I heard a nervous murmur as vampires and werewolves hurriedly scattered to clear the space around me. I glanced over my shoulder to see a familiar face.

Roland strolled up behind me with calm, measured strides. He wore a grim frown and he was covered in blood. His shirt was ripped open from one of his skirmishes, revealing the huge crucifix branded across his muscular torso. He assessed the sinister building with a critical look. "Big ward," he murmured.

The naked woman cleared her throat. "We've surrounded the building so the demons can't escape, but we do not know if any children survived. Dead bodies litter the foyer, so it seems unlikely."

Roland and I studied the building, and I knew he was doing the same as me—checking for distant heartbeats. He was better at it since he had more experience, so I nobly chose to let him show off for the crowd.

"None of you have guns?" I asked the naked woman. She and the others shook their heads with guilty grumbles. I sighed in frustration. "Go to the abandoned gun shops and arm up, but leave money on the counter or make a list of what you take so we can pay the owners back later. We are not looters."

The werewolves let out excited whoops and then they were trotting down the street—a squad of wolves and naked people—to raid any nearby armories.

I stared up at the building and gave a slow nod, feeling the rain wash over my face and cheeks. "How many?" I asked Roland.

"Five," he said. I reached into my satchel and counted my collection of Tiny Balls. I only had four of them, but they were connected to Castle Dracula. Although that destination would likely be frightening to children, orphans were tougher than most and it was safer than remaining here as hostages or playthings for demons.

I cocked my head and looked over at him. Whatever he saw in my face, he stepped back. "Give me ten minutes and then follow the trail of bodies."

He clenched his jaw but finally gave me a curt nod. I stepped up to the ward and felt my skin pebble and tingle as the air vibrated warningly. I reached out a finger and tentatively touched it. My skin slipped through the ward and I bit back a gasp at the iciness that seeped directly into my finger bone. But nothing alarming happened. I stepped through, feeling like I'd just plunged through a sheet of ice in a polar bear challenge.

Then I was through.

11

The place was vast and as silent as a tomb. The stone ceiling was a complicated diagram of arches and curved domes with stained glass skylights thirty feet overhead, reminding me more of a Renaissance or medieval church than any kind of orphanage. I was surprised a private company hadn't bought it to transform into a niche, ritzy hotel. With the black clouds filling the sky, only the faintest beams of anorexic light managed to shine down through the upper windows, just barely hitting the cold marble floor of the foyer before dissipating. As such, darkness lurked in the corners like living wraiths waiting to pounce.

The heavy rain created a steady drumming sound against the roof and the windowpanes. The very air and walls felt sinister and lifeless, giving off a vibe of remorseless hateful truth to the residents of the orphanage: *the world didn't want you and doesn't care about you...deal with it. Your tears are probably why your parents abandoned you.*

Maybe I was just projecting my own nightmares from childhood, but they did resonate with this place. I felt an instinctive flush of anger and I desperately wanted to burn this building down to the ground, leaving only dust, ash, and rubble in its place.

Like you did to Abundant Angel Catholic Church, a sinister voice whispered in my ears. *Like you did to the other 'orphanage' that took you in?*

The worst part was that the voice wasn't Envy since I had sent her to

Solomon's Prison. The taunting voice was entirely my own. I shuddered and took a calming breath. Children were in danger and I was supposed to be here rescuing them, not wallowing in my own childhood insecurities. I opened my eyes again and studied the place more critically, doing my best to abandon my emotions and leave my personal passions out of my assessment.

Facts, not feelings, Callie, I encouraged myself.

My shoulders itched like I was being watched, and I knew there was almost no chance that a child sent here would ever leave with any semblance of normalcy or hope. Whatever spark of life they might have still carried upon entering this place would have eventually been snuffed out and replaced with a flame of hatred. No wonder a demon had zeroed in on this place as a nice second home.

A pretty yet morbid dungeon. A beautiful cave of death.

Not a safe and loving refuge for abandoned children. This was a place that would nurture them in violence and suspicion and cynicism.

The air smelled of fresh blood and gore.

A statue of an angel occupied the center of the foyer as a divine center-piece to symbolize protection.

One of the house mothers had been crucified on it.

Metal spikes had been driven through her wrists into the angel's outstretched wings, fully supporting the woman's dead weight. The angel was smiling benevolently, and someone had used the woman's blood to emphasize the statue's caring smile into a devilish grin, a la the Joker in Batman. Even if she had been terrible at her job, she hadn't deserved to go out like that.

I swept my murderous glare across the rest of the large lobby, checking the grand staircase for threats or signs of life. The broad steps were garishly decorated with statues of praying children backed up against either railing, creating the depiction that the children were worshipping those who used the stairs—which was likely the person in charge of the place since the lobby was likely not intended for the veteran orphans, only the newcomers. It was disgustingly narcissistic, in my opinion. The place was a mess—unkept, dated worn furniture from a few decades ago, and it was so dusty that I could see the motes drifting in the air.

I walked on silent footsteps like Ryuu had taught me, keeping my head on a swivel as I drew my silver katana—I didn't want to announce my presence with the fiery swords in the gloomy building. I held the weapon high, wary of a potential ambush. My boots tingled warningly but I hardly needed them these days—I would be more worried if they were *not* tingling because they seemed to always be stuck in the *on* position any time I set foot in Kansas City.

I reached the base of the stairs, keeping my eyes alert for any sudden movement, but I was forced to do a double-take for a closer look at one of the kneeling statues on the stairs. I froze and my sword arm started to tremble as I stared in abject horror. My eyes suddenly burned like I'd been sprayed with tear gas and my pulse spiked as what felt like a cold weight settled over my shoulders.

They weren't statues. They were orphans.

On every other step, a child in tattered, stained linens knelt in a pool of their own blood, their hands bound together by barbwire and lifted to their own foreheads in a mockery of prayer. Their hearts had been torn out of their chests and neatly placed in their laps.

In that moment, I decided that not a single creature in this place would receive a quick death. I sheathed my katana; the velvety whisper was barely louder than my breathing.

I reached into my satchel and pulled out my new toys from Hephaestus' ornate chest. I tucked the chest back into the satchel and gripped my new accessories with an expectant smirk on my face.

I lifted my silk scarf over my mouth so that only my eyes showed from beneath my hood. Then I strode up the stairs like a ghost, breathing a silent prayer for the dozens of dead children I passed.

Your protectors failed you, but your avenger is here, children, I thought to myself.

I reached the upper landing and tucked myself close to the wall, using my vampiric hearing to check for dangers. I heard nothing in my immediate vicinity, so I risked a quick glance around the corner to make out a long, wide, shadowy hallway that definitely reinforced my thoughts on the gothic cathedral motif from the foyer. In the distance, I heard faint bickering and grumbled laughing, but the hall between us was dark and lifeless—

A sharp cry rang out, piercing the silence like a gunshot. A child.

I reacted on instinct and sprinted down the hallway with a silent snarl. My scarf snapped against my cheeks and one of the tails whipped free of my hood to trail behind me in my haste. The hallway had to stretch fifty feet into darkness, and I had covered half its length before my eyes registered a demon standing in the center of my path. He was looming over a whim-pering child, gripping a fistful of her hair as he held a claw to her delicate throat. Except he was grinning at me, looking entirely too smug—

I spun around just in time to reflexively deflect a cudgel swinging for the back of my head. Specters of distorted, demonic shadows came to life all around me, forcing me to use my peripheral vision and instincts to defend myself. I shoulder charged the cudgel-wielding demon and sent him clat-tering to the ground where he bowled over at least three other demonic shadows who had all been hiding in the alcoves on either side of the hallway. Within seconds, I was on defense from what had to be a dozen lesser demons—black rather than the usual red—as they attacked me en masse.

The child hostage had been bait to lure me out.

I lunged forward with one hand to grab a demon by the horn and then I punched him in the face as hard as I possibly could. Blazing bright light flared from Hephaestus' freshly forged, blessed brass knuckles. Bone and horn cracked. Blood sprayed.

I laughed.

He squealed.

His legs buckled but I kept a firm hold of his cracked horn and then I hit him again on his way down, crushing his orbital bone with another flash of holy light. He crumpled completely to the ground and then I stepped on his face for leverage as I twisted his horn until it broke free with a satisfying *snap!*

I spun the demon's horn into a reverse grip to use as a dagger and I turned to face the other demons, who were now climbing back to their feet. I lifted my fists in a boxing stance and grinned. "Put up your fucking dukes, devils," I drawled.

They stared at my metallic knuckles with bewilderment, anger, and fear, and it had nothing to do with their fallen brother's horn clenched in my fist. My knuckles were glowing with crimson light in the stark gloom. Well, my flashy new bling glowed in the darkness.

Both sets of brass knuckles had been forged from melted crucifixes and cooled in Holy Water. They had no magical properties, but they were forged in faith, blessed with prayer, and baptized in the blood of Christ.

Which tasted strangely similar to Welch's grape juice, but that's neither here nor there.

I'd told Hephaestus to make many, many more, and to give a set to anyone and everyone who could safely wield them—you know, without bursting into flames or anything. My vampires would have issues wielding them, obviously, but Roland and Samael were working on a way to help them temporarily overcome their aversion to Holy relics.

I stared at the lead demon. "You're about to have a very bad night. Hope you said your prayers." Without waiting for him to respond, I spun to face the demon I had sensed trying to sneak up behind me. I stomped down on his pitchfork just as it was lunging for my lower back, causing the forks to stab into the floor with a flash of sparks that knocked him off balance. I crouched and then used every ounce of my strength to give him a rising uppercut to the jaw that elicited another flash of blessed light in the dark hallway, setting off a chorus of hisses from his fellows as they wilted away from the presence of God. I hit him so hard that he flew up into the ceiling and his horns stabbed into a wooden support beam, getting him stuck. He started kicking his legs wildly, whimpering and snarling.

I grinned at my creation. "A demoñata!" I crowed as I went to work on his body with my blessed knuckles, treating his lower ribs like a heavy punching bag, except with more sizzling hisses of cauterized flesh, impotent cries and grunts, and the splintering *cracks* of pulverized bones.

Someone tackled me from behind, but I spun on instinct and managed to deflect most of his momentum so that he ended up horn butting his punching bag ally, goring his ally demoñata's stomach open from left to right and spilling the poor bastard's intestines all over the floor. I slipped in the sudden shower of gore and promptly fell—hard—on my ass bone with a sharp flash of pain and a bestial grunt. Three demons promptly dogpiled me, smothering me in writhing, scaly bodies.

I gasped and struggled for air as I clawed with my hands to latch onto anything I could use for leverage, but the puddle of fresh blood only served to lube us all up like we were in a Greco-demon wrestling match. We slipped and slid all over ourselves in an effort to get the upper hand. An arm slipped into my grip and I immediately hyperextended it with a focused strike from my other hand. He screamed and thrashed wildly, knocking his fellows away and clearing me a space. I sucked in a breath of fresh air and kicked another demon in the teeth. Two follow-up kicks shattered every black fang in his maw as he let out a gargling cry. Then I head butted the last demon in the nose, sending up a gout of demon blood into the air. With the strange ward around the orphanage, I doubted I would be able to drink his blood to get a power up—not that I would have wanted to anyway.

I rolled to the side and received three kidney punches before I cleared the tangle of furious, wounded, slippery demons. I scooped up a discarded pitchfork and started wildly stabbity-stabbing like a sugared-up child playing Whac-A-Mole. I was panting hoarsely by the time the last wrestling opponent stopped thrashing. I spun in a circle, wielding the pitchfork in a defensive pose, but there were no more demons in sight. Had I really killed them all or had the others fled upon witnessing my berserker genomes taking the steering wheel?

I saw a side door that was cracked open and I heard the echoes of racing hooves coming from beyond. I tore forward and yanked open the door to find a dingy stairwell hugging opposite walls to double back on itself as it stretched upwards and downwards. Dim emergency lights cast the space in a hellish red glow. A demon stood in my way, looking startled at my lack of cautious pursuit. I kicked him in the groin as hard as I could.

I'm pretty sure I heard the sound of two squishing grapes upon contact with my foot. Testicles now popped or propelled somewhere up into his esophagus, he squealed and stumbled down the stairs, knocking over another pair of demons guarding the next landing. I ran down the stairs as one of the victimized demons managed to regain his hooves just in time for me to bury my pitchfork into his throat and pin him to the wall hard enough to permanently wedge my weapon into the aged brick. I let out a frustrated curse as I let go of the haft of the ironic weapon and then I stomped on the nut-tapped demon's deflated scrotum for good measure.

I reveled in his shriek of hellish agony.

The second demon received twin blessed knuckled fists to the lower ribs, causing him to double over with a grunt...where he was introduced to my knee to his jaw. I palmed his face and shoved, causing us to half-fall down the next flight of stairs. I used his body to cushion my fall and managed to slam the back of his skull into the wall twice before someone tackled me from the side and sent me tumbling down the *next* steps.

I landed on my back and banged my head on the ground, but I managed to kick my assailant—the neutered demon, apparently—up and over me, sending him flipping out into the open space between the descending stairs. I heard the resounding *ping* of him hitting a railing a few floors down, and then—a few long moments later—the sound of a smashed watermelon echoed up from far below as he hit the bottom floor. I wheezed desperately, blinking up at the zig-zagging stairwell that climbed much higher than I would have thought for an orphanage. After a few moments, I grasped the railing with bloody fingers and pulled myself to my feet, panting wearily.

The staircase was silent—except for the gurgling demon still choking on the pitchfork in his throat.

12

I shambled down the shadowy stairs as I checked the pistols in my shoulder holster. I was surprised they hadn't fallen free or been snatched up by one of the demons. Maybe they weren't familiar with guns. "Okay, Callie," I rasped out loud. "No need to go Frank Castle on them and get yourself killed for a pop culture reference," I mumbled, spitting out a mouthful of blood. "That's a Nate Temple tactic. Be a good Catholic like Matt Murdock. They know not what they do."

I finally reached the lowest level and all but collapsed against the wall with a weary sigh. I took note of the motionless demon splattered across the center of the floor next to me. Where his head should have been was now only grisly gore and two severed horns.

I grimaced and closed my eyes for a count of three as I struggled to catch my breath.

"I can rest after I get the kids," I whispered to myself. Then I hesitantly pressed my ear to the door—trying not to recall that fatal bathroom stall scene from *Scream 2*—to see what awaited me on the other side. I heard nothing and my boots weren't buzzing as much as before. I spit out more blood, gritted my teeth, and then I opened the door. I slipped into a cozy space with peeling, floral wallpaper that could have only been picked by a grandmother. It looked like a shared living room for several connected dorms, and the decor had never been intended to appeal to children of any age. In my peripheral vision I saw an elevator to my right and dated, utterly boring paintings in gaudy, gilded frames on every wall. Maybe it was a teacher's lounge for the resident workers. A fire crackled from a fireplace against the back wall, and a few couches and chairs formed a semi-circle seating area that faced the doorway I had just entered from. Despite the strangeness of having a stairwell open directly into this room rather than into a hallway that might *lead* to a room like this, it wasn't the weirdest thing about my present situation.

I wasn't alone.

Creak-creak. Creak-creak. Creak-creak.

An old woman was seated in a rocking chair, calmly rocking back-and-forth as she stared at me without surprise. Despite looking like a malnourished, geriatric, serial killer-slash-baker, her eyes glowed with yellow flame and her liver-spotted hands featured long black claws ripping through her fingertips. A frightened little girl with short, curly red hair sat on her lap, doing her best not to move for fear of the claws gripping her shoulder.

Two smaller children, a handsome dark-skinned boy and a mousy, pale-haired girl, sat on the floor on either side of the rocking chair, hugging their knees to their chests as they silently sobbed. They were nine or ten and they wore collars made of bulky black metal. Two red-skinned henchmen demons loomed a few paces behind the seated children, and they held black chains that were connected to the kids' collars. Leashes. They'd leashed the children.

I narrowed my eyes at the demonic old woman and wiped some blood from my chin. "Call me Mommy Warbucks. I'm here to ruin your day, Miss Hannigan." I scowled at the two red demons. "That makes you Lily and Rooster. I'm about to put your insides on your outsides unless you drop those leashes in the next five seconds."

The two demons pursed their lips anxiously but the old woman bubbled out with a jubilant, grandmotherly laugh before waving a reassuring claw at her henchmen. Her beady yellow eyes locked back onto me and she smiled warmly. "So, you are the infamous White Rose. I have heard *so much* about you."

In my mind, I continued to count down from five, even as I nodded to the old woman. "It seems my name is on everyone's lips these days. Granted, it's usually with their dying breaths. 'Why did you impale me with my own horn, White Rose?' 'How could you sever my hoof and then beat me with it,

White Rose?'" I waved a hand absently. "Comments along those lines." I eyed her up and down thoughtfully, stroking my chin between my thumb and first knuckle. "Do you have any doilies? I haven't killed a demon with one of those yet. Reputations must be meticulously cultivated and nurtured with fresh corpses to remain healthy and strong."

She hissed at me and I folded my arms with a big ol' grin.

...two...one.

I remained motionless but I suddenly focused all of my attention directly on her and let my smile disappear in an instant. My body language was so intentional and abrupt that I felt the three demons stiffen with healthy concern as I stared directly into grandma demon's eyes. So, no one noticed when two of my silver butterflays silently shimmered into existence directly behind each henchman demon and then dive-bombed their lower spines to rip through their stomachs like drill bits. The demons squealed and dropped their leashes as their bellies exploded, spilling blood and guts onto the floor between them and their captives. They fell to their knees, shrieking as they grasped at their ruptured stomachs. The kids screamed in fear, but I had eyes only for the shocked look on the old woman's face.

My butterflays landed on each of her knees and began slowly flapping their blood-soaked wings open and closed as butterflies were wont to do.

But the matriarch reflexively looked over at her gored demons and completely overlooked the lethal butterflays that had landed on her knees, likely wondering how the hell I'd hurt her henchmen without moving and without using my wizard's magic. Orphan Annie noticed the deadly butterflies with bulging, wondrously terrified eyes, looking afraid to even breathe. In the matronly demon's growing panic and confusion, she shifted her grip on orphan Annie's shoulder just enough for me to make a risky decision. I sent a silent command to my butterflays.

They zipped upwards and sliced cleanly through grandma demon's wrists, severing the deadly claws as surgically as a scalpel. They fell to the side and one of them stabbed one of the thrashing henchmen in the eyeball with a disgusting *pop*. The henchman let out an ear-piercing shriek as he frantically reached up to grab his boss's severed hand and remove it from his orbital cavity.

The other hand landed on the ground and twitched spastically in a phantom gesture as if hoping to slice Orphan Annie's throat. Meanwhile, Miss Hannigan screamed as her stumps sprayed blood in every direction, realizing she'd literally been disarmed. I lashed out with a tendril of magic as her jaws gaped impossibly wide in an attempt to bite Orphan Annie's head off. I yanked the girl free of danger and into my arms, giving her a swift, reassuring hug before I shoved her behind me. Miss Hannigan's jaws clicked shut on empty air and she rose to her feet, her eyes latching onto the other two children in collars. The dark-skinned boy abruptly kicked out with his foot and struck her in the side of the knee. The mousy girl scooped up one of the severed hands and slammed the claws into Miss Hannigan's chest with a feral scream.

Miss Hannigan snarled and collapsed back into her rocking chair with a furious and agonized cry. I heard the rocking chair creak alarmingly but it didn't break under her weight. I yanked the other kids back to safety with two tendrils of air around their ankles. The three of them huddled together in relief as the shock of adrenaline raced through their bodies, but I was already racing forward with my right hand held back over my head.

Miss Hannigan looked up at me with surprise as I tackled her in a flying monkey leap to straddle her lap and obliterate the rocking chair. We crashed to the ground in an explosion of splinters and shattered wood and I rode her down to the ground where the back of her head slammed into the tile near the fireplace. Her bloody stumps swatted at my back and sides and she tried to bite me with her long wicked teeth, but I took a firm grip of her hair with my free hand and then leaned close enough to feel the rush of air against my cheeks from her snapping teeth only inches away.

"We love you, Miss Hannigan!" I snarled in a sing-song tone. And then I punched her with my blessed knuckles, cracking her forehead hard enough to make her eyes momentarily roll back as her head slammed back down to the tile. The skin on her forehead sizzled upon contact with my blessed knuckles and when I hoisted her head back up, I grinned at the brand burned into her forehead—which I had been unable to observe on the foreheads of my foes in the darkened hallways and stairs.

WWJD smoldered across her forehead in a hasty brand.

I reared back to punch her again when I registered someone gagging behind me. Then I heard the subdued, muffled whimpers of the children. I pursed my lips and glared down at the dazed demon. Then I summoned up a blade of magic and severed her head to make sure she couldn't hurt anyone ever again.

I turned to the huddled children and gave them what I hoped resembled a cheerful smile—despite the blood all over my body—and held out my arms. "You three are incredibly brave. Thank you for helping me stop them. My name is Callie."

The dark-skinned boy scuffed his foot on the ground and averted his eyes. "We didn't do anything. You saved us all by yourself."

I smiled warmly and crouched down low so that I was head-level with him. "I've seen grown men pee their pants when they confronted their first demon. Did any of you pee your pants?" I asked sternly.

They laughed and shook their heads.

I focused back on the boy. "You not only kept your head, but you struck a counterattack as soon as you saw an opening." I met each of their eyes and nodded solemnly. "Most would have simply run away at the first opportunity. That is bravery...even if you did *feel* like peeing your pants in the moment," I added with an impish grin.

They grinned reflexively, though it was short-lived. "But I was terrified!" the red-headed girl whispered.

I nodded and then shrugged. "I'm frightened all the time. Especially these days," I told them. "But fear and bravery go hand-in-hand. Being brave is when you *overcome* your fear and stop letting it control you. Fear is useful, but it must always be your servant."

I glanced back at the dead demon and recalled the general aura of the place. "They were not kind to you here, were they?"

All three children shook their heads without hesitation. I wasn't sure if those in charge had been cruel humans who merely provided a nurturing habitat for the demons to possess, or if they had always been demons. It was too late to ask any of them. The red-headed girl looked up at me and her face paled. "Does this mean we're being sent away again?" she whispered, even as she snatched her friend's hand as if to deny the chance they might be separated.

I folded my arms and pursed my lips pensively. With the current war taking place on the streets, I doubted I would even be able to get someone here to watch over the children—almost all of the Regulars had fled the city. But...Castle Dracula was relatively safe now, thanks to the Toymaker's Guardians and Xylo's rapidly growing army. It was safer than Kansas City.

I studied the three children thoughtfully. "Have you guys ever seen a castle?" They shared a long look with each other and finally shook their heads. I smiled warmly. "Do you want to?"

They grinned excitedly and nodded.

I rose to my feet and nodded. "Then let's get out of here." I turned around and scooped up the demon's severed head. Maybe Envy could tell me who it had been. It was a long shot, but better than nothing. Especially if she had the power to put up the ward around this place. If demons started wielding power like that, we were in for some serious trouble.

I used the old bird's hair to tie a knot around my sword belt. I shifted the dangling head to my hip opposite my sword, and then I motioned for the children to follow me as I made my way towards the stairwell door. "All ready?" I asked. They nodded nervously. I opened the door and entered the stairwell of death.

✿ 13 ✿

They followed in silence, giving me a safe buffer to battle any new demons that might jump out at us. The stairs were dim and smelled of blood, but they were seemingly empty. No ambush waiting for us. I still wore my blessed knuckles, and I kept my hand on the hilt of my katana just to be sure as I started climbing the first few steps, motioning for the children to follow me.

"It won't take long," I assured them. "Hold hands and don't be alarmed when you see the dead bodies."

"Dead bodies?" Annie squeaked. The three children murmured collectively as they huddled closer together, forming a chain of holding hands.

I nodded absently, knowing my level of alertness was far more important than my level of compassion and empathy in our present circumstances. Plus, these were hardened orphans. What they had seen downstairs was far worse than the mess I'd left behind here. But I did feel tension in my shoulders as I crept up the steps. The fact that I was now protecting children rather than looking out for myself gave the dim, bloody, twisting stairs a much more sinister ambiance.

The children followed my wary, cautious, slow-as-molasses pace without complaint until I paused with a frown. We were one level below the exit to the main floor I had used earlier, but something wasn't sitting right in my gut. I sniffed the air warily and reached out with my senses to see if I could pick up on a heartbeat or anything that might announce a threat. But that wasn't what had set me off. Something was wrong with my thoughts. I felt like I had left my car keys downstairs or something. I glanced down at my waist to make sure I hadn't left a weapon behind.

I saw nothing missing so I pursed my lips, taking note of my boots, the bloody smears on the floor, the discarded pitchforks, and the utter absence of dead bodies—

My eyes bulged in alarm. "Shit," I whispered. I looked up sharply to scan the rest of the stairs both above and below us. Blood everywhere but not a single dead body from my earlier violent rager. I even saw the pitchfork still buried in the wall from where I'd stabbed it through the demon's throat. I spun to face the children with a hopefully reserved but insistent look on my face. They stood on the landing in the middle of a large pool of blood from my earlier fight, and they stared back at me with wide, terrified eyes, trembling enough for their shoes to create faint ripples in the puddle of blood. "We need to hurry—"

The weak emergency lights flickered and I froze. I narrowed my eyes and scanned the stairs stretching high above me with a critical eye, but nothing moved and the lights stayed on. I let out a weak laugh and plastered on a faux smile for the kids. "It's okay," I lied, realizing we had stepped into some kind of trap. "Let's just get out of here—"

There was a sharp clanking sound and then the lights turned off entirely, almost like someone had thrown the master lever on the circuit breaker.

I gripped my katana and scanned our surroundings, cocking my head for any source of noise that might herald claws on stone, heavy breathing, or any other moderately threatening sound. I heard nothing so I let out a soft breath and crouched down to get on level with the children and reassure them—

They were gone. Completely *gone*.

"CALLIE!" Annie screamed from a few levels below me. "HELP!"

Thankfully, my vampire senses gave me better night vision than most people, so I was able to see a dull monochrome outline of the stairwell, complete with black splotches marking the blood.

I was running back down the stairs with my katana out before I consciously realized it. I split my attention between the bloody floor and the space ahead, wary not to run into a trap. I was staring down at the ground on the next landing when I abruptly skidded to a halt as the hair on the back of my neck pointed straight up. I stared down at a relatively clean section of ground following a sizable puddle of blood. My footsteps could clearly be seen trailing away from the puddle.

But...

There were no other footprints leaving the puddle. I checked another puddle behind me and one ahead of me—they revealed the same thing. Only *my* footsteps.

"Motherfucker," I snarled, drawing my katana. "I almost fell for it, you rotten little shits!" I called out into the darkness. My voice echoed in the stairwell. I held my breath and kept my head on a swivel, expecting a horde of prepubescent demons to dogpile me.

Then I heard a sound echoing up the stairwell, growing louder with each passing second.

Laughter. Creepy laughter. It made me feel like I had woken up in the middle of the night to get a glass of water and found an antique porcelain doll sitting in a creaking wooden rocking chair in the center of a gloomy room that had been entirely empty hours before. Then the laughter doubled in on itself as one of the other children joined in. Then it tripled, growing louder and much, much closer.

I spun around and rabbited up the stairs. "Fuck this place!" I hissed.

I grasped the door handle and flung it open, panting desperately as I blindly swung my katana left-to-right in front of me. I felt no resistance on my blade and I opened my eyes to see no demons nearby. The door to the stairs slammed shut behind me, buying me a moment of reprieve. Besides the stench of death and sulfur, the hallway reeked to high-heaven of something sharp and cloying, but I couldn't quite make out what it was with my senses focused solely on the creepy ass laughter still racing up the stairwell behind me.

I hopped over the bodies of the demons I had killed earlier and raced for the entrance, breathing heavily. I had no idea why these bodies remained when the others had disappeared, and I truly didn't want to learn the answer. I skidded to a halt as I neared the lobby, because a silhouette rose up from a crouch, squaring their shoulders to face me head-on. Of course, the door to the stairwell behind me exploded and the three demon children screeched with murderous glee as they burst through and zeroed in on my location to attack me from behind.

I stared at the tall silhouette and realized it stood atop a mound of fresh corpses and my rage suddenly ignited. Had my allies tried to enter the building only to be slaughtered by this son of a bitch on the landing? I stared through the darkness between us, trying to use the flashes of lightning through the skylights above to get a clear look at exactly what kind of demon I was facing, but they stood just within the same hallway as me, so the flashes of light did me no good. Without breaking eye contact, I drew my pistol in my free hand and started blindly firing behind me at the lying, raging, shrieking demon children. They snarled and screamed furiously but they kept right on coming.

The silhouette in front of me lifted a small, familiar-looking cherry of light to its face and I realized its hand was shaking with exhaustion at the effort. I frowned as I let off a few more shots behind me, shifting my aim from left-to-right. The silhouette took a trembling puff from a cigar, and the cherry glow illuminated a blood-soaked, furry face with large blue eyes and unmistakable whiskers.

I let out a breath of relief but kept on firing behind me. "Grace!" I rasped, feeling like a weight had been pulled off my shoulders. "When did you start smoking cigars, and what the fuck are you doing in here?" I wheezed. "You could have just said hi!"

The Easter Bunny shambled forward a few unsteady steps, looking like she'd been freshly raised from the dead. "Callie," she whispered in a shaky tone. "I got twelve of the murder munchkins," she wheezed, pointing back at her pile of bodies. She took another deep puff of the cigar and I was thankful for the sweet scent's ability to almost obscure the acrid stench in the hall. Did decomposing demons let off a different stench? I'd never really hung out long enough to find out. "The dead ones on the stairs weren't as dead as I thought," she added with a growl.

I realized what was wrong with her voice. She was angered and shaken by the fact that she'd had to kill children. Although they were demons, the Easter Bunny had been forced to kill kids.

I had no such compulsions after what I'd seen. Evil little shits had made me feel sorry for them.

I popped off a few more shots behind me—the ensuing cry let me know I'd hit pay dirt—as I risked a glance at the stairs. They were empty. No more posing dead kids holding their own hearts in their supplicant palms. I shuddered involuntarily, wondering how such a thing was possible. Had the kids been possessed after I walked past them or had they been lying in wait for my return? I also saw a few discarded red containers I hadn't noticed on my way into the orphanage.

Grace nudged my shoulder with her paw and I flinched to see her waving a second cigar in front of my face. I opened my mouth to argue and leaned my head back, but she took it as an invitation to shove the cigar into my mouth. Having no hands to defend myself, I bit down on the cigar so it didn't fall and burn me. "Let's burn this motherfucker down, sister." Then she drew the second pistol from my shoulder holster and started firing over my shoulder as she tugged me towards the stairs and away from the hallway.

I awkwardly sheathed my katana and turned to face the pursuing children as we walked backwards towards the stairs. I stumbled over one of the red containers and almost fell on my ass before Grace steadied me. I frowned. "Wait. Are those gas canisters?"

Grace exhaled a cloud of smoke and I heard a familiar clinking sound of a zippo lighter as a tall flame sprang to life in her free paw. "Merry Christmas," muttered the Easter Bunny with a cynical smirk. And then she flung the lighter into the hallway and it erupted in flame so bright and hot that I felt the skin of my face suddenly tighten and shrink.

The demon children squealed in croaking, bubbling, sizzling horror, and then the inferno blasted out of the hallway and into the lobby, hitting us with a shockwave of force as unexpected and swift as a dickpunch from God, sending us tumbling down the stairs. I banged my shoulder and knee hard enough to cry out, and then we were lying on the floor of the lobby, staring up at the gaping holes in the ceiling where the skylights had been. Rain poured down through the openings and into the building in a steady stream that looked almost like struggling waterfalls as they reflected the orange flames on the upper level hallway. Lightning crackled across the sky with great thunderous booms and Grace burst out laughing, even though it sounded like it hurt for her to do so. I twisted my head to find her lying beside me, and I watched as she took a great big puff of her cigar. Her fur was covered in blood and I saw a few fresh scratches on her cheek and upper arm, but she was relatively unharmed. I was surprised to find I still clamped my own cigar in my teeth and that it hadn't been broken or sent flying in my rapid tumble down the stairs. I took a big puff and immediately started coughing and hacking.

Grace turned her head to glance over at me with a big toothy grin and then climbed to her feet with a weary groan. "Come on, sister. We have a reputation to uphold and those hairy chested brutes outside are going to storm in here any second to make sure us weak womenfolk are okay." She frowned down at her paw and cursed. "Shit. I broke a nail," she muttered with an annoyed growl.

Then she sighed in resignation and held out her paw to me. I pulled myself to my feet with minimal grunts and hisses, even though my shoulder throbbed and my knee felt swollen. I glanced up at the blazing fire at the top of the stairs and grimaced before shaking my head. "Fucking children."

Grace nodded and handed me the gun she'd borrowed. "Poor bastards," she agreed. "Look," she suddenly said, pointing her cigar up at the entrance to the hall. A singed, horribly burned bat-like creature awkwardly crawled out of the flames, making mewling, whimpering sounds before collapsing to their side. I realized Grace had a throwing knife prepared to hurl at the demon child, but she sheathed it once it became apparent that the creature had died from its burns. "Well, let's go face the music," Grace said, turning her back to the flames and the rain pouring through the ceiling. She glanced down at my side and arched a quizzical eyebrow. I looked down to see the old demon's head still firmly tied to my belt and the WWJD brand stamped into her forehead. Two of her front teeth were missing from the fall. Grace burst out laughing, doubling over. "What would Jesus do?" she hooted.

I smirked and shrugged. "Well, he probably wouldn't have done any of this," I admitted with a sigh. I grabbed her wrist and pulled her towards the door. "Thanks for having my back, Grace."

She wrapped a bloody arm around my shoulder and took another puff of her cigar. "None of those pansies outside seemed inclined to do it."

I nodded. "I told them not to. Roland was going to check on me if I took too long."

Grace gave me a faux innocent smile. "Funny how he sent me in here *before* the deadline. Finding a way to break your order without breaking your order."

I smiled faintly as I pulled open the door to find a curtain of pouring rain. Roland stood a few feet away, ignoring the rain pounding down on his head and shoulders as he stared unblinkingly at me. Seeing me moderately safe, he dipped his chin with a faint smile. I glanced over at Grace. "He's kind of an asshole like that," I agreed.

But I was smiling. Cantankerous, old, overprotective bastards were sweet in their own annoying way. Roland correctly interpreted my scowl and puffed out his chest triumphantly. I threw my cigar at him and relished in his reflexive flinch and shout.

Like the infamous *Twist and Shout*, but better.

❧ 14 ❧

I let out a sigh of relief and relaxed my shoulders to see the same werewolves and vampires as earlier now forming a protective detail around the building. The building continued to burn, but it was mostly made of stone, so I wasn't too concerned. The rain would help keep it in check. Cain was crouched on the sidewalk a few paces away with his back to us, looking focused on something in front of him.

I eyed her up and down curiously. "Is any significant amount of that blood yours?" I asked.

She waved her cigar at me. "Nothing I can't handle. I wasn't able to move as fast as usual thanks to their little protective ward. Most of the blood belonged to…" she trailed off with a sickened glance at the orphanage and shuddered. "Those poor bastards," she said with a twinge of sorrow and guilt.

Roland stepped up beside me and I could tell he'd been listening in because he didn't immediately start berating me for lighting the orphanage on fire. In fact… "Hey," I said suspiciously, "who's idea was the gasoline?"

Roland winced guiltily. "Mine. Heard from Ryuu about similar situations on the other side of town. Turning the hostages into the enemy and using them as bait to set the trap." His eyes settled on me. "A trap for you, of course." He glanced down at the severed head on my belt and his face flushed crimson upon noticing the brand on her forehead.

"Blasphemy is a victimless crime," I told him defensively.

He grunted noncommittally and looked over at the burning orphanage. Clouds of black smoke now rose up into the air through the broken skylights. The building was definitely a lost cause with no active fire department to help shut it down. I hadn't been certain that the building proper would actually catch. The halls had been mostly stone and the rain pouring inside should have helped deter the spread, but Grace was an ambitious little bunny. She must have doused the furnished rooms off the main hallway.

I walked towards Cain with a thoughtful frown. "What are you doing?" I froze as his arts and craft project came into full view. He was inspecting one of the wandering angels. A dead demon looked to be next in his forensic analysis.

He glanced up at me and gave me a grim smile. Then he used a long dagger to lift up the wandering angel's cuff and show me the bare wrist. "I was curious whether they had those same shackles as the nephilim."

I nodded grimly. "We aren't that lucky. I've seen these things attack a pair of stray dogs."

Cain grunted and rose to his feet, sheathing his dagger and then brushing his palms together. The rain continued to pour down on us and I lifted my face to the sky and closed my eyes, taking a deep breath as I felt anger broiling dangerously hot within my chest. The falling water felt like it sizzled when it struck my cheeks so I doubled down on my breathing until I felt a hand grip my shoulder.

I reflexively flinched and snarled as I hopped back a step and drew my katana. Cain arched an eyebrow with his hand hovering in the air where it had been touching my shoulder. He slowly turned his palm towards me in an appeasing gesture. "I think you're ovary acting," he carefully enunciated the words with a lopsided grin.

I blinked at him a few times, wondering why he'd enunciated it so strangely. Then I got it and I let out a groan of disapproval. But I felt a smile struggling to split my cheeks as I shook my head and meekly sheathed my katana. "Sorry. I'm just a little on edge," I admitted.

"You should be burned at the stake for that one," Grace muttered to Cain, but she was also smiling.

Cain bowed graciously and then flashed his teeth in a victorious grin. "You're welcome." Then he turned to me. "We should get you out of here, Callie."

Grace warily scanned the nearby rooftops. The burning orphanage was reflected in her big eyes and I winced. I'd have to do something about that. Grace finally turned back to me. "He's not wrong, Rosie. You have been out for longer than normal, and the Horsemen are determined."

She'd given me the nickname once she'd learned about Envy's moniker, the Black Rose. I clenched my jaw and shook my head. "I'm sick and tired of hiding. We're not actually accomplishing anything by putting out these tiny fires of resistance." Cain and Grace pointedly stared at the burning orphanage and then turned back to me. "Figurative fires," I amended.

They carefully and politely argued my point, but I sensed Roland watching me pensively. I tuned them out and found myself staring down at the corpses Cain had collected. The wandering angel wore dirty robes that had once been elegant and white. They were now blood-stained at the hem, singed in many places, and generally ragged and stained. Even the baptismal rain was unable to wash away the filth—unable to absolve them of their sins.

As Cain and Grace continued arguing—seemingly with each other now—I crouched down over the wandering angel, feeling my anger coming back tenfold. These creatures were supposed to be good and pure and noble and virtuous. Viciously steadfast, but primarily good.

The demons did not hide behind such flimsy veneers. In a way, they were more honorable by owning their vices. These mysterious wandering angels used their supposed virtue as cudgels, smiting with abandon after their abrupt arrival into the realm of men. Had they Fallen—capital F—or had they been knocked out of Heaven in some sort of coup at the Pearly Gates? They had seemed horrified—shellshocked, actually—to find themselves down here, so it definitely hadn't been voluntary. I had momentarily hoped that an army of allies had been sent down from Heaven to aid us in the upcoming war, but I had been quickly corrected when they tried to kill us on our first rescue mission.

Before I consciously realized it, I observed my dagger methodically sawing off one of the wandering angel's wings. The dagger was connected to my white-knuckled fist and it wasn't trembling in the slightest.

"Um..." Cain began, standing a few feet away from me and looking slightly concerned. "Whatcha' doing?"

"You ever hear that nursery rhyme, Ring Around the Rosie?" I asked them. Cain grunted affirmatively.

Grace sang out the next lines. "Pockets full of posies. Ashes, Ashes, they all fall down."

I nodded. "Your nickname for me. Rosie."

She frowned down at the wing. "Posies are flowers, right?"

I shrugged. "Posies were actually bouquets of flowers given as a gift, but it's the thought that matters. The gift. These are a kind of bouquet. I'm sending a message," I told them calmly. "Saw off the demon wings for me."

Silence answered me. Well, silence and the continuation of falling rain and burning orphanages, broken only by the bright flashes of lightning and sharp cracks of thunder. Without a word, Grace and Roland leaned over the demon and got to work sawing off a wing each. Cain crouched down across from me, met my eyes for a brief moment, and then he let out a resigned sigh. He began sawing off the other angel wing just as my knife tore through the appendage. I picked it up in one hand and then rose to my feet.

I walked into the center of the street and used my foot to lob a pitchfork up into the air. I caught it with my free hand and then called upon my magic to empower me as I slammed the pitchfork down into the asphalt. The tips sank down through the stone with a metallic clang at a depth I was sure could not be easily removed.

I set the severed angel wing on the ground and calmly untied the severed demon head from my belt. I lifted it to my face with a clinical assessment and then I clenched my jaw. "This bitch killed children or worse," I murmured to myself. Then I slammed the head down onto the base of the pitchfork, impaling the grandmother demon. I scooped up the wing and then slammed it into the temple of the severed head hard enough for it to stick out sideways. Cain stepped up on the other side and mimicked my action, slamming the other white angel wing into the demon's other temple so that it looked like she had giant Dumbo-sized angel wings for ears.

Grace and Roland stepped up to me and eyed my work with blank but slightly nauseated looks. I held out my hand expectantly and waited for Roland to hand me one of the black feathered wings. I ignored his caring, imploring look, giving him only a cold, no-nonsense stare in return. He nodded his understanding and gave me the wing. I checked the severed base of the wing and saw a sharp protrusion of dark bone. I nodded my satisfaction and stabbed the wing down into the top of the demon's head, breaking through her skull so that the wing stood straight up vertically.

Grace gave me her wing and I promptly stabbed it up through the soft palate beneath the chin, turning the art piece into a Holy and Unholy wind-mill. It couldn't spin or anything, but it served my purposes.

Callie Penrose and company were here to stay and alliances would only be made on my terms.

I walked up to the front of my work and made some adjustments before taking a few steps back to assess it in its entirety. It was horrifyingly beau-tiful to see the elegant white and black wings pincushioning the grandma demon's severed head, but the WWJD brand truly stole the show. I nodded satisfactorily.

I heard a sharp commotion behind me and I turned to see one of the Seven Sins and an Archangel calmly walking towards me. The werewolves and vampires formed two lines of warriors, forcing the two brothers to walk between them. Of course, the walls merged together behind them, trapping them in a crowd of angry, antagonistic, deadly monsters. The brothers didn't seem entirely concerned with the danger but they did take respectful note of it as they approached me.

I'd first encountered Gluttony at the now-infamous Dread Wedding. Gluttony hadn't been the biggest asshole and he also hadn't been interested in overcompensating to intimidate and bully anyone. If anything, he had seemed entirely disinterested in the actual conflict between everyone, finding more interest in the potential for rewards after the fighting was over. Of course, as soon as Ryuu's trap had been sprung and all my murdered allies had come back to life—courtesy of the Dueling Grounds expansion—Glut-tony had promptly decided that the festivities were over. He'd been hanging out with Lust on the sidelines, watching the mass murder while eating popcorn.

To see him with an archangel was shocking in itself, but to see him with an archangel I had not met was downright alarming. Where was Raphael? Supposedly, there were Seven Archangels for the Seven Sins. Gabriel was bromancing somewhere with Wrath, I'd taken Michael for myself, and I'd killed Uriel. So...which of the three other brothers was this, and why was he strolling around with his archenemy? Literally.

Gluttony halted a safe distance away from me and then pointedly leaned to the side to look past my shoulder. I stepped clear and held my arm out in a flamboyant pose like I was revealing a glorious work of art. Then, noticing that I still had blood on my hands from my earlier work, I turned to look directly into the stranger archangel's eyes, smiled wolfishly, and then I popped my finger into my mouth to lick off some of the blood. The power instantly shot down my tongue, electrifying my muscles and joints like a blast of adrenaline and I only just barely managed to contain my gasp of euphoria. Had mixing the angel and demon blood supercharged it or something? It would make sense.

They might not know it, but angels and demons were two parts of one whole—an Anghellian.

It obviously wasn't common knowledge to anyone, but a few of them seemed to know—and they kept it to themselves. I'd revealed that secret by merging Michael and Lucifer back together with their grace in purgatory. When Gabriel and Wrath had learned this, they promptly fled like the brave badasses they were known to be.

Bitches.

The archangel didn't look impressed by my windmill. Gluttony let out a long whistle and then settled his hands on his hips as he shot me a roguish grin. "Whoa, chica," he purred in a surprisingly sexually charged tone. It didn't seem to be intentional or specifically directed at me; it was just a seductive aura he exuded. "You, um, busy?" he asked with a very warm and inviting smile.

The archangel sniffed primly, not bothering to hide his disapproval. Gluttony rolled his eyes but kept his words to himself rather than chastising his holier-than-thou brother.

I smiled at the Sin, preferring to ignore the archangel entirely. "Are you asking me out to dinner, Gluttony?" I asked in a sultry purr as I slipped another blood-soaked finger into my mouth.

He shifted from foot-to-foot, seemingly caught off guard by my tone or gesture, I wasn't sure which. "Um. Well, I wouldn't say I'm *not* asking you out to—"

The archangel interrupted him with a silent but furious glare and Gluttony rolled his eyes in resignation. The archangel shifted his poignant stare to me. A flash of disappointment crossed his face when I didn't flinch or cower in the slightest. He sneered at me and then started speaking in a haughty, bitter, disdainful tone, "You have been summoned—"

I turned my back on him with a derisive sniff and approached my newly-made altar. I brushed my fingers across the angel's feathers in a fond gesture. "I don't answer *summons*. But I have been known to consider formal requests when they sound moderately entertaining, but only when I have absolutely *nothing* else to do," I said in an absent tone.

"On pretty letterhead," Grace added, and then she let out a jaw-cracking yawn.

I didn't look up from my altar, but I did lift a hand to point my finger at her in acknowledgment. "Yes. That."

The pattering rain was the only audible sound for a few awkwardly silent moments. "Did you bring a formal invitation on pretty letterhead?" I heard Grace ask, her voice dripping with syrupy sarcasm.

More silence answered her, and I heard the two brothers murmuring back and forth. Finally, Gluttony cleared his throat. "No formal invitation. But it wasn't a summon—er, request," he corrected, "to meet with *us*. We're just the messengers."

I paused, staring down at the wingless bodies a few paces away on the sidewalk. Then I burst out laughing. "A nameless archangel and a Sin are messengers? For who?" I chuckled, shaking my head. "Messengers usually carry messages."

"The Four Horsemen," the archangel replied, sounding both embarrassed of his lowly role yet mildly triumphant at what it might mean for my future.

❦ 15 ❦

I wiped my brow with my sleeve, feigning a lack of concern even though my pulse had spiked at mention of the Four Horsemen demanding an audience with me. I was about ninety-nine percent certain they wanted to execute me, and about one percent certain they wanted to torture me first. I still didn't understand why they were so fixated on my alleged crime of using my Dread Four mask against Greed—some kind of Horseman United Nations rule I'd flagrantly broken—especially when they showed zero concern for the crimes of the people they were actually supposed to be regulating—Heaven and Hell.

They were using an archangel and Sin as messenger pigeons for crying out loud. What the hell was all this really about? They were terrorizing my city and seemingly working with each other as often as not. Were humans the real enemy to them and they simply had differing views on how to exterminate us? Weren't the Biblical Four Horsemen supposed to help humanity to some extent? If not, what was their true purpose? I knew Revelations told of them wiping out large swaths of humanity, but they supposedly did so on behalf of Heaven. Right?

I made sure my features were composed, and then I turned back to face Gluttony rather than the archangel. "Let's put a pin in the whores' sons for a minute," I said dismissively. The archangel sputtered furiously as if I'd blasphemed against Creationism itself. "Take a girl out to dinner first, Gluttony. I'm sure you know a few good spots."

The archangel hissed like a startled snake. "They are waiting right *now!*"

I ignored him and folded my arms as I continued to stare at Gluttony. "I'm only getting hungrier," I said conversationally.

He risked a glance at his compadre before casting a mischievous smirk my way. "Yeah. I know a place or two. What kind of food do you want?" He glanced at Grace thoughtfully. "Any dietary restrictions? You're not vegan, are you? This is barbecue country."

She snorted. "Definitely not a vegan. To be fair, I think butchers are gross, but people who sell vegetables as full meals are grocer." Gluttony burst out laughing and Grace curtsied with an imaginary dress as she cast him a wicked grin. "I want to hear my pulled pork squeal, boy. Wooo pig! Sooie!"

I grinned at the Easter Bunny. "I knew we were friends for a good reason."

"We are *not* getting dinner!" the archangel snapped. "The Horsemen are waiting!"

I rolled my eyes. "I have it on good authority that they have no authority over me," I said.

A second archangel swooped down from the sky and landed beside his siblings. Raphael cast me a wary glance, gauging the physical distance between us as if to verify his own immediate safety while hoping to placate my anticipated aggression. A dark shape leapt off a nearby roof and slammed down onto the ground with a superhero pose that broke the pavement around her. Lust rose up like a stripper finishing her routine and batted her eyes at me.

"Did I hear you call them whores' sons?" she hooted approvingly. "They are *so* pissed."

Raphael shot me another cautious look to make sure I hadn't devolved into a primal beast intent on attacking him from behind. He shifted his gaze to his brother archangel. "What is taking so long, Ramiel?"

The archangel—Ramiel, apparently—pointed at me. "She says she wants to go to dinner first. "

Lust glanced at my creation with a mildly startled look on her face. "I hate to break it to you guys, but I think the White Rose is closed to the idea of making friends with us. Any of us." She appraised me pensively, no longer looking as nonchalant as a few moments before.

I shrugged. "As the Bible says, live as long as I let you live. Corinthians 1:87."

Ramiel frowned. "That's...not in Corinthians."

Lust snorted. "It's not even from the fucking Bible, you imbecile. It was a threat, sweetie. Let's call it Exhibit B for my earlier point about her not wanting any new friends."

"I could have sworn that was Corinthians 1:87," I said with a dismissive shrug. "But I'm not a very good Catholic."

Gluttony grinned. "Quite a few Romans in town would agree with that statement," he drawled, referring to the Shepherds and the Conclave. I didn't mention my private meeting with their leader this morning. It was actually a relief to learn they weren't aware of it—they hadn't been spying on the Vatican camp.

Roland stepped up beside me and let out a hungry growl. "Italian cuisine is one of my favorites," he said with a wicked smile. "When in Rome, eat the Romans...cuisine," he said, pointedly pausing between words.

Grace stepped up on my other side and frowned. "I only kill people that look at me sideways," she said with a shrug.

Both Sins and archangels looked uneasy of my squad even though they showed zero concern for the werewolf and vampire swarm behind them.

I smiled at the winged siblings. "I'm working on reducing the Shepherds' numbers at every opportunity, but don't worry. I hold the same special feelings for you guys as well," I said, gesturing at both sides of the family.

Raphael pursed his lips and I saw his eyes subconsciously shift to the katana at my waist, remembering how I'd whooped his ass outside the Garden of Eden a few days ago. I grinned and gave him a slow, knowing nod. He blushed and let out a long sigh. "Perhaps we should dispense with the veiled threats and do as she requests. Trust me. It would be better for everyone. Whatever we need to do to get her to the meeting."

Lust clapped delightedly. I smiled and dipped my chin at Raphael, but Ramiel looked like he'd been punched in the forehead. "*What?*" he hissed. Raphael pulled him aside for a private conversation and I found Lust and Gluttony watching me with amused grins. I was curious how much honesty and humility Raphael would share with his brother about the result of our sword fight, but they muted their conversation with some...Kumbaya magic or something.

I turned my back on them and wrapped an arm around Grace and

Roland's shoulders. Cain watched us curiously, close enough to hear as I spoke no louder than a whisper. "Home sweet home. On my signal."

They masked their reactions perfectly and gave me faint nods of understanding. I detached from them and turned back to the siblings, confident that my crew knew what to do.

The four of them were watching me suspiciously but their alarm faded to see that my shoulders were relaxed and not discreetly drifting towards a weapon. My allies were similarly relaxed. I walked up to Raphael and smiled brightly. "You coming to dinner?" I asked him sweetly.

He studied my face and gave me the faintest of nods. "Yes."

I smiled brightly. "Good." I turned to Gluttony and Lust. "Lead the way." They stared at me pensively before Gluttony finally shrugged and started walking down the street.

I sidled up beside Raphael and took note of Ramiel's openly suspicious looks. I arched a cool eyebrow at him. "Do you mind?" He grunted and gave us some space. I stared at him until he took another step away with a muttered growl. Then I turned to Raphael and smiled. "I think we got off on the wrong foot."

He studied me sidelong, obviously wary of our close proximity but not wanting to look fearful in front of his brothers. "Well, I think you blatantly proved that I was on the wrong foot, to say the least," he admitted, glancing down at the hilt of my katana.

I laughed and nodded. Then I extended my elbow to him. "Truce?" He hesitated and I let out a sigh. "There are four of you and only one of me. I'm sure you could make short work of my entourage if you worked together," I said, arching a curious eyebrow.

He considered that and finally relented. He hooked his arm into the crook of my elbow as if he was escorting me to a ball. We continued walking down the rainy streets and I took a deep breath, appreciating the humid, clean air. I felt his posture relaxing and I smiled as I pointed at Lust and Gluttony bickering ahead of us. Raphael followed my finger and smiled very faintly. Then he glanced over at me sidelong and he looked troubled. "I don't understand you, Callie Penrose. Which side are you on?"

I chewed over his question. Even I wasn't entirely sure how to answer it honestly. In the spirit of our truce, I gave him the truth. "The people of my city. I'm a defender of my people, but the barbarians are at the gates."

He narrowed his eyes. "We are not barbarians." He tensed slightly and guided me to the side, skirting a puddle on reflex.

I grinned in surprise. "Awwww. That was actually sweet of you, barbarian," I teased.

The corner of his lips curled up and he scoffed. "I am not a barbarian," he repeated.

I leaned closer to whisper conspiratorially. He smelled of cinnamon and spice and all things nice. "What about Ramiel? He seems like a bureaucratic dictator. Like an angry, one-man HR department." Raphael coughed to conceal his obvious agreement and Ramiel glanced back at us with a suspicious frown. Raphael's countenance instantly changed and he shot Ramiel a furious glare. His brother archangel wilted and his spine stiffened as he turned away. He may as well have yelped like a whipped dog.

Grace chuckled from behind me and I heard Cain murmur something that made Grace laugh even harder. Ramiel stiffened even more and stomped through a puddle harder than necessary.

I shot Raphael a questioning look and he shrugged. "Hierarchy."

I squirreled that comment away for later and gave him a thankful nod. "Well, I think we can agree that Uriel cracked and became tyrannical. Barbaric, perhaps."

Raphael grew eerily silent. "So it would seem."

Which was more than I had expected him to admit. "What about Gabriel? What is his goal here? Why did he betray Michael, who was simply trying to do his job? It seems each of you have a measure of free will that I hadn't anticipated. Maybe more free will than even you archangels realized."

Raphael hesitated. "There is much we do not know, or were incorrectly led to believe. That does not make us barbarians."

I nodded and reached over with my free hand to pat his forearm affectionately, getting him used to my touch like he was a skittish horse—which he was. He tensed but allowed it. "This is nice," I told him, taking another deep breath of the rainy air. Thunderstorms were my favorite weather, but this one was dying down now. Regrettable.

"What you did to those demons and angels was barbaric," he said in a neutral, surprisingly non-judgmental tone.

I nodded. "Principles and courtesy don't win wars against mindless savages. I don't have to like it, but I won't run from it. Sometimes we have to get down into the muck to make a point. Sowing fear and confusion are powerful weapons for the times when nobility fails. Virtue and flowery, idealistic phrasing sounds pretty on an elegant, embossed invitation to an elaborate event, but war is a symphonic orchestra of violent vices that assaults everyone in the audience."

He chewed over my words for a few moments and finally nodded. "So, you have abandoned your virtue?"

I laughed and then shot him a lascivious grin. "Oh, honey. I abandoned my virtue long ago."

He frowned, not getting the joke for a few moments. I licked my lips and kept right on grinning. His eyes abruptly widened. "Oh. That...that was *not* the subject matter, Callie Penrose!" he sputtered.

"*Now* it is," I said, chuckling. "Hey, Lust! Come here for a moment. Raphael wants to learn how to lose his virtue—"

Raphael stammered an objection as Lust glanced over her shoulder and shot him a smokey look.

"She is twisting my words," Raphael argued. "I do not wish to lose my virtue. We are fine," he said sternly, glaring at her until she turned back to the front with an amused laugh. He shot me a dark look. "That was also barbaric," he said stiffly.

I leaned in close and patted his forearm with my fingers again. "Now you're getting it." He subconsciously guided me away from another puddle and I smiled guiltily. "You are much kinder than your brothers, Raphael," I admitted, almost sadly.

He picked up on my tone and frowned. "You offered a truce. I am honoring it," he said with a perplexed expression on his perfect face—his angelic mask that hid all the scars underneath.

I sighed and patted his forearm again in an appreciative touch. "Sucker."

Then I Shadow Walked the pair of us out of Kansas City against the archangel's will.

I heard the shattering of Tiny Balls as my allies responded to my impromptu signal and fled. I also heard the beginning shouts of protest from Raphael's siblings before the rainy street disappeared from view and perfect darkness swallowed us up.

Then the mighty Archangel Raphael attempted to fight back, ripping the blackness to ribbons of light. I screamed as I experienced the sensation of my flesh being peeled from my bones.

I think Raphael screamed even louder, though.

✿ 16 ✿

In the bowels of time and space, there was no beginning and no end. Just an infinite loop of chaos.

We screamed until our throats were raw, and we flipped end-over-end, entwined in mortal embrace as we fought for dominance over the other. Raphael had somehow disrupted my attempt at Shadow Walking him to a specific destination, and now we were both caught in the riptide of creation.

Shadow Walking was typically an instant trip from point A to point B.

Raphael's intervention had caused us to miss our exit and we were now on a cross-galaxy road trip.

Stars blasted across my vision as we momentarily wrestled through a midnight black sky as cold as death and without oxygen. It winked out before I could even process the thought of us being in space and having no air to breathe. Then we were crashing through a rainforest, sending a troop of monkeys screaming and scattering as they swung through the trees to escape. Light flashed out all around us, burning and freezing beams of energy as Archangel Raphael fought the scrappy White Rose. Next we crashed into a snowbank and I felt my lungs freezing solid before we shifted to a sweltering, desolate world of scorching sunlight and an impossibly expansive blue sky. We slammed into a solid sandstone wall, and I was fairly certain I caught sight of the broken sphinx statue as we tumbled and fell down the side of a giant goddamned pyramid.

I felt Raphael drawing on his power as the world blinked out of view again, sending us to a place so bright and humid that I slammed my eyes shut for fear of blindness. Instead of continuing to react, I summoned up every power I could imagine and blindly tried to stop Raphael from...

Well, whatever the fuck he was trying to do. I wasn't even sure if he knew what that was, because he sounded just as startled and alarmed by each shift in location as I felt. I might have even heard him utter a naughty word, which I would definitely use against him later.

If we survived my snafu of a kidnapping.

Raphael's power threatened to swarm me, but I fought back with my wizard's magic. I didn't have a connection with Sanguina since she was still on extended family leave, and I knew I couldn't draw upon my Mask of Despair because the Four Horsemen felt very strongly about me using my special toy to fight this war.

The Dread Four only had jurisdiction over the *other* pantheons, and the Four Horsemen viewed me playing in their Biblical sandbox as the equivalent of uncovering a hefty deposit of still-warm catshit in their sandcastle's throne room.

I felt Raphael beginning to overpower me, so I did the only thing I could think of. My silver vampire fangs extended from my gums and I bit him as hard as I could, sinking them in deep. Unfortunately, during our topsy-turvy tumble, we'd gotten into a physical tangle that made his ass cheek the closest available target for my bite. Had I known this minor detail beforehand, I would have waited for a better opportunity.

Such is life. Like a guard dog to a postman, I locked my jaw and owned my shame.

His power evaporated in an instant and he let out a horrified squeal. "YAHWEH!" he shrieked, imploring the Almighty's aid. The ridiculousness of the situation and his cry for his Daddy almost made me lose my grip, but I wrapped my arms around his waist and held on for dear life.

I clamped down like an atheist mongoose wrestling a Catholic cobra.

His blood hit my mouth like I was hearing a choir of divine trumpets and my body convulsed at the explosion of energy that suddenly ripped through me.

I became light—infused with the assblood of the Holy Spirit.

I was power. Everything else seemed inconsequential. Even my own body felt ephemeral and imagined. My soul had risen from my mortal shell and I felt I could do anything. I used that power to swamp Raphael's futile attempts at struggle and I blindly reached up to grab his halo with my free hand.

I grasped repeatedly at empty air, funneling the power of his archangel blood into my attempts because I wasn't using the Omegabet to help me like I had with Envy and Greed. I heard a sharp cracking sound and his body went rigid like he'd been nut-tapped by a lightning bolt. The icy metal ring materialized against my palm. I gripped it like my life depended on it and I felt his body go limp as he let out a gasp of air.

Followed by a long squeaker from his sphincter.

I gagged and reared back, struggling to hold my breath from the Archangel's potential death curse.

We slammed into a metal fence that hadn't existed a moment before. My shoulder popped upon impact, but Raphael struck it face-first, hard enough to break his nose and snap him out of his unconscious stupor. I managed to maintain my grip on Raphael's halo even as my world spun from the abrupt halt to our astral travels and we crashed to the ground. I was forced to squint at the sudden brightness surrounding us.

I let go of his waist and grabbed at the metal fence to support my weight, fighting back against the throbbing pain in my shoulder as I struggled to make sense of our surroundings.

"Oh, no," Raphael wheezed, sounding horrified. He didn't try to fight me but the fear in his voice was strong enough to make me shudder.

"Don't even think about running away. You farted on me, you son of a... well, that wouldn't make any sense," I mumbled woozily. "You bastard," I amended, blinking rapidly as I scanned the strange environment.

"Archangels don't fart," Raphael argued vehemently.

"Women came up with that lie," I muttered, but my anger swiftly faded as I realized we stood in a hilly valley of sorts. Except the ground was made of clouds and the sky was purple. I frowned uneasily as I slowly turned my head to look at the metal fence I was leaning on. It wasn't metal.

It looked like...pearl.

I stumbled away as if it might be electrified, dragging Raphael away in the process. He was meek and obedient even though he was obviously panicked. I was still gripping his halo and it seemed that Raphael had heard all about my hobby for collecting the cursed rings.

I licked my lips nervously as I looked up and up and up at the colossal white gate. "Where...are we, Raphael?" I asked softly. Very, very softly.

He sounded numb and almost robotic. In the grips of despair—literally, as it were. "The Pearly Gates," he whispered.

I slowly nodded at the confirmation of my fear, and then I glanced from left to right, noticing other sinister landmarks. "Why are the gates covered in blood and feathers?" I whispered. "And who are all the dead people?" Mounds of mutilated body parts and gore made eerily neat little piles all around us, as if someone had cleaned up after an epic battle. I saw plenty of wings, both black and white, in the piles.

Raphael was silent for a long moment, sounding like he was sobbing. "This must be what broke the angels in Kansas City. Why they fell. Why they turned into wild beasts."

I shook my head in disbelief. "Who could assault the Pearly Gates?" I whispered. "What if they're still here?"

Raphael craned his neck to look up at me. His face was bloody and his mask had fallen away to reveal a scarred but still relatively handsome face. His nose was now broken and bleeding freely, but it was those damning, haunted, hopeless eyes that almost—almost—made me release my grip on his halo.

"I'm more frightened of what the invaders may have unintentionally unleashed," he rasped, pointing to a small berm of cloud. A liberal blood trail led behind it as if the victim had tried to hide behind it. I dragged Raphael close enough to get a brief glimpse. My eyes settled on several huge, scaly piles of shredded meat and black feathers. I instantly gagged and backed away until it was out of sight again. It had either been several powerful demons or one extremely powerful demon dissected into what looked like mounds of ground meat.

"What...the fuck did *that*?" I gagged.

Raphael shuddered. "Cherubim or Seraphim."

I swallowed audibly. I'd heard of them but I hadn't learned anything useful other than that they were powerful. My second useless bit of trivia was that famous historic painters had depicted cherubs as chunky babies with bows and arrows and adorably pudgy cheeks.

If cherubs were capable of this level of violence, the Renaissance painters —ironically named after a few of the Seven Archangels—had obviously depicted falsehoods in their masterpieces. There was a conspiracy afoot, but I didn't have time to fire up the Dan Brown signal.

Raphael lifted a shaking hand and pointed out dozens more of the piles dotting the cloudscape. The number of dead angels and demons seemed relatively equal, and the carnage continued on past the Pearly Gates on a stairway of clouds that led dozens of stories upwards where it ended at a humongous Gateway of crackling purple light.

Except black smoke was drifting out of it and I saw fingers of red lightning within the massive Gateway, as well as floating black clouds. I turned to see Raphael staring at the same thing, and he looked like his entire world had been turned upside-down. He was in shock.

"I'm guessing Heaven is not supposed to look like that?" I whispered.

He shook his head stiffly. "No." He stared woodenly at the impossible view.

"I'm just spitballing here," I began, "but that looks more like a depiction of Satan's anus than a doorway to paradise."

❧ 17 ❧

Raphael nodded woodenly. "It is all over. My home has been destroyed..."

I frowned down at him. "Hey! Get your shit together, archangel! How do you think *I* feel? You farted near my face and kicked off the Apocalypse."

"I don't fart," he argued sternly. My quip must have lit a tiny fire under him because I sensed his figurative spine growing back as his fear slowly submitted to his rage. "And this happened long before we arrived." He took a calming breath and turned to sweep his furious gaze across the clouds. He froze and I followed his gaze to see him staring at a specific pile of bodies.

I glanced over at him. "Please don't tell me that's the famous baptist," I murmured, feeling my stomach roil.

He slowly shook his head. "No. John is a fighter. If he's anywhere, he's up there," Raphael said in a frozen growl as he pointed towards Satan's anus at the top of the distant stairway to Heaven. "Or he is dead. The only way to release the Cherubim and Seraphim is with his keys."

I frowned. "What? They were locked up? How the hell does that make any sense? This is supposed to be Heaven for crying out loud."

He slowly turned to look at me as if I were daft. "The Cherubim and Seraphim are practically forces of nature. They know only war. Their sole purpose is fighting during the Apocalypse. They are not...tame," he finally said, choosing a word that only seemed to moderately satisfy him. But he did assess me with a critical eye. I still gripped his halo, so his glare felt like a physical attack due to our proximity. "Why are your nephilim here, I wonder?" he asked in a murderous tone, pointing at a tangle of bodies that looked more human than the rest. "How did we wind up here at the Pearly Gates if you haven't been here before? I know I did not pick this location, and I was in no position to control our destination at the end of our journey," he declared as he subconsciously reached back to massage his asscheek.

I narrowed my eyes dangerously. "I've never been here before!" I argued incredulously. "I wouldn't even know where to *start* to find this place!"

He folded his arms and stared unblinkingly into my eyes. "Yet here we are. You executed Uriel and now hold the fiery sword. Thunder and Terror are yours to wield. Uriel could have told you how to get here. The information could have been tortured out of him if you used the sword against him. I experienced your skills firsthand. If you could best me then you could easily defeat Uriel, and he could definitely lead you here." He glanced down at my hand and his eyes locked onto Envy's black halo. He sneered. "Or perhaps your new roommate wanted vengeance and used you to destroy everything I love."

I jutted out my jaw and opened my mouth to argue with him, but rather than uttering a word, I swiftly kneed the Archangel Raphael in the nuts. He dropped to his knees with a whistling whine and I rolled my eyes. "Boys are so predictable." I let out a frustrated breath and glanced back at the supposed nephilim he'd spotted. I'd need to get a closer look to be certain, and I wouldn't have put it past Raphael to try and get me worked up enough to make a mistake and release my grip on his halo—his leash. "The moment I returned from the Garden was when the angels started falling from the sky. Whoever did this waited until I was preoccupied with you and Uriel at the Garden. The timing is absolutely perfect," I murmured, more to myself than the wheezing archangel. What if...Uriel had been a distraction? Could Gabriel and Wrath have done this? Would they have done this? Why bother with Kansas City if they intended to assault Heaven itself?

Raphael was regaining his composure and finally lifted his head to glare at me. "Swear to God you didn't do this," he said in a no-nonsense tone.

I arched an eyebrow at him before pointedly glancing at the chaotic Gateway at the top of the steps. "You want me to swear to a God that didn't protect his own paradise...that I didn't attack said paradise?" I asked drily.

He pursed his lips at my blasphemy so I let out a sigh and squatted down before him. "If I had the ability and power and knowledge to orchestrate such an attack, I wouldn't also be the kind of girl to bite an archangel's ass or let an archangel mess up my attempted kidnapping. I wouldn't have even needed to kidnap you in the first place if I could do that," I said, pointing at the purple Gateway.

He studied me intently, reading my eyes in silence.

I let out a breath and gave him a sympathetic smile. "Sorry for trying to kidnap you, Raphael. I wanted to show you something but I knew the others wouldn't let you leave without an escort, and I couldn't risk them learning what I wanted to show you. I don't know who else I might possibly be able to trust. I'm not saying that I trust you, but we do seem to share a love for honor. You learn a lot about a man in a sword fight."

His jaw tightened, but not in anger. He looked...surprised.

I released his halo to show him my sincerity and then I rose to my feet. "I don't know how we got here, but I'm almost one-hundred-percent certain that whoever did this is a raging dickhead. I fight raging dickheads."

I held out my hand invitingly and he stared at it as if waiting for it to sprout claws and slice his throat. After a few beats, he clasped my forearm and pulled himself up. "We are not on the same team," he said firmly.

I gestured at the surrounding carnage. "You sure you don't want to rethink that? I could say the enemy of your enemy is your friend, or I could remind you that of the four Archangels I've spent any considerable time around, Uriel is dead, Gabriel was working with Wrath and fled after I outplayed him, Michael joined my team, and the last one got his ass whooped in a sword fight—yet he's still standing next to me right now."

Raphael pursed his lips unhappily. "Ramiel makes five."

I shrugged. "Today was the first time I met him. Give me time."

"The Sins have had similar outcomes after meeting you," he added.

I rolled my eyes. "Wild theory here, but maybe your family is dysfunctional," I said. His eyes took in all the bloodshed around us and I wished I could take my words back. I hadn't been referring to this, but it only served to emphasize my point. "You've seen what working independently has earned us. I think new tactics are in order."

He considered my words and then let out a soft breath. "No guarantees."

I pointed towards the nephilim he had indicated. "Are you sure those were nephilim?" I asked as I started walking in their direction. He nodded and followed suit.

"They had the cuffs. One gold and one black."

I grimaced at mention of the black cuffs. I still didn't know who had given them to the nephilim or what their purpose was. Removing the golden cuff—when that was all the nephilim had worn—had broken their blind servitude to Heaven, but when Grace had removed both cuffs from one of the nephilim at Castle Dracula, the nephilim had dropped dead on the spot. I pondered this as we walked across the clouds—a ridiculously surreal sensation, but only when you stopped to consider it. The surface was slightly spongy but not sticky like a swamp. It was strangely beautiful and mesmerizing—I almost tripped and ate it but I managed to catch myself at the last second. Raphael covered his mouth in a bullshit cough.

Stupid fucking clouds and asshole archangels.

We passed entirely too many piles of shredded meat that had once been neatly sausage-wrapped in skin or scales, but now resembled masticated pulled pork. I kept my eyes up and tried to avoid the crimson-stained sections of clouds, reminding myself every three steps that they were not cherry cotton candy.

We finally reached the bodies and I grimaced. Once again, they looked so mutilated that it was impossible to tell what they had once been, but I saw two severed hands protruding from the top of the pile, and they each had a cuff—one black and one gold. The hands belonged to two different nephilim; one was black and the other had a deep bronze complexion.

I sighed, shaking my head. "My nephilim don't wear the cuffs, Raphael. They are free." I gritted my teeth and removed the cuffs from the severed hands. As soon as I retrieved them, I quickly turned away and took deep breaths to prevent myself from throwing up. I slowly turned to look at him. "You know, free from the chains your brothers put on them," I said, holding the cuffs out to him.

His scarred face tightened but he didn't comment on the veracity of my claim. He also didn't try to deny it. He stared at the bloody cuffs in my palm and let out a frustrated breath. "The black cuffs came from the Conclave. I don't know what they are, but they give off a similar power aura as the golden cuffs. What I'm more concerned about is how they got here in the first place. Secondly, how we came to be here."

I pursed my lips and slipped the cuffs into my satchel to inspect later.

Maybe I could figure out how to remove them from a living nephilim without killing him. "I tried Shadow Walking us somewhere else entirely, but when you started fighting back, everything went all crazy on us. We globe-trotted when we shouldn't have even been able to leave Kansas City."

He frowned. "If we weren't able to leave the City of Fountains, why did you attempt to Shadow Walk?"

I smiled mysteriously. "I made the red dome over the city," I lied, "and I know the only way out of town."

He brushed a loose strand of hair from his face and eyed me critically. "I see."

I looked back towards the Pearly Gates and Satan's asshole at the top of the stairway to Heaven. "You feel up to confronting whatever is going on up there?"

He considered it longer than I thought he would, and I felt my respect for him grow. "It would be a waste of our lives. We need to tell others what we have learned. We need to find out what we're up against."

I watched him in silence, neither agreeing or disagreeing with him.

He grew noticeably uncomfortable under my quiet scrutiny. "I am not afraid to die, White Rose, but Michael taught me never to win a battle at the expense of the war. We would die here with our foolish vanity and honor intact, and the world would pay for our pride."

I smiled at the irony. Pride—Lucifer—was Michael's new roommate, but I didn't want to annoy Raphael any further. We were making progress in our relationship. Instead, I held out my hand. "How about we go for that ride I initially attempted? Maybe don't fuck with the space-time-continuum this time."

He grunted and grasped my forearm. I Shadow Walked us to a world of fire and sand.

⚛ 18 ⚛

I hadn't noticed how chilly the temperature was at the Pearly Gates until it was replaced by the flame-throwing-sand-blaster temperature of the arid Sahara desert. "Welcome to the edge of the world, Raphael."

The blistering sun bore down on us and my throat felt dry as dust. I lifted my scarf over my mouth to prevent chewing on sand, and I motioned Raphael to follow me towards a circle of separate tents covered by a camou-flaged canopy that would theoretically conceal us from aerial surveillance—angel or human. But the Sahara desert was huge, and no one knew we were even here, so the risk was minimal.

Even with the patchy shade of the canopy, it was still hot as balls.

Sand dunes stretched as far as the eye could see in every direction but one, which was blocked by a swirling, inverted vortex of black, crystalline sand. Strangely enough, it made absolutely no noise, looking like a massive, hazy pyramid. It was rooted to one specific spot, and that was what had brought us here. The Divines had found it two days ago after Xuanwu and Starlight had scoured the astral plane in search of Sanguina or any other strange anomalies. This was why I had made a secret exit in the dome over Kansas City, so we could crack this particular chestnut.

Because I was pretty sure that Azazel and Samzaya were inside it. Unfortunately, the Divines hadn't figured out how to get inside yet, and every camel test subject had been shredded in seconds.

I wondered how long it would take Raphael to notice the silent behemoth behind us.

One tent was loaded with supplies—water, clothing, armaments, first aid kits, foodstuffs, and cooking equipment. The other tents were sleeping quarters and a mess tent for eatings or meetings.

Three men were playing cards around a folding table outside the mess tent. A tall handsome man in a muscle-tank and linen pants rose up at our arrival and stared at us. He had the beginnings of a blonde beard and he wore black Ray-Ban sunglasses. I stared in confusion. "Cowabunga, Raph!" Lucky bellowed.

"Shut up, Mikey," Raphael muttered in a familiar manner. Then he stiffened and stared at Lucky in confusion. "Michael?" he whispered. "I thought Uriel had killed you!"

Lucky peeled off his shades and grinned at Raphael. "I'm my own man now, brother, but I'll always have my memories," he said, tapping his temple.

He looked the same as when I had last seen him before his transformation—human. His long golden hair was tied back in a man-bun—probably the infraction that had gotten Lucifer sent to Hell in the first place—and he wore a bro-tank that said *Jesusaurus Rex*. His irises were now metallic yellow like molten gold rings.

I stared in disbelief. "You're not a golden dragon!" I blurted.

"Three six's," Alucard drawled from the card table, more interested with their game than my arrival.

Lucky ignored my comment and spun towards Alucard with a triumphant laugh. "Go fish! That is *literally* the first time that phrase hasn't pertained to me! Is this what it feels like?" he asked, seeming deliriously happy at the innocuous revelation as he patted his chest and thighs excitedly. "It's amazing," he said in a wondrous tone.

Alucard lifted his sunglasses with one finger and eyed Lucky strangely. "I don't get it," he said. "What's amazing?" He turned to the last man at the table, Gunnar Randulf. "Did reptile Jesus get into Starlight's edibles again?"

"Better not have!" I heard Starlight's voice bellow out from within one of the nearby tents before falling into a fit of giggles. Strangely, I heard a handful of feminine giggles echo him, followed by a bunch of other inappropriate sounds. From within the enclosure, a furry arm with red manicured claws yanked the flap of the tent closed, muffling the amorous chorus.

This place was supposed to be a secret operation, and Starlight had brought drugs and a harem. Of course.

Gunnar looked like the leader of a Viking biker gang. He too wore sunglasses and he was biting down on a massive cigar. His white eyepatch glinted in the bright sun and he wore a collared linen shirt that was unbuttoned down the center, showing off his ridiculously broad chest. He held his cards fanned out before him as if there was real money on the line rather than the reality that they were playing a children's game. Two of the big bad Dread Four were playing Go Fish with the born-again Devil.

To be fair, Lucky had attempted to explain to me that Lucifer hadn't been the Devil-devil. His name had become synonymous with the supreme asshole, Satan. It could have been a lie or it could have been the truth, and I wasn't sure which would be worse.

Gunnar shot Alucard a look of resigned disappointment. "Six-six-six. Lucifer. The Devil," he murmured before pointing at the stack of cards in the center of the table. "The Devil told you to go fish," he reminded Alucard.

Alucard grunted unhappily. "I thought that was Jesus' catchphrase."

Gunnar snorted and I caught a whisper of a smile beneath his beard. "Not these days." Gunnar let out a tired sigh and tossed his cards on the table. They made a strange clanking sound and I realized that they were camping cards, made of some kind of metal so as not to blow away in the wind. "Forty-five games is my max anyway," he said, finally turning to look at me. He did a once over, pursing his lips at my general state of affairs—blood covering my hands, mouth, and likely my pale hair—before shifting his intimidating gaze to Raphael. He casually twisted his neck from side to side, eliciting a string of deep cracking sounds. Then he rose from the table in an overly casual manner and folded his beefy arms across his chest. Gunnar was tall and huge, but something about his mastery of the murder-glare made me realize that he could have lost a hundred pounds and he would have still scared most people he encountered.

It wasn't that he was violent and threatening. He was just…immovable. Resolute. He was like a statue of Hercules after completing his infamous labors.

"Quitter," Alucard grumbled, but he sounded relieved to stop playing.

I snapped my fingers pointedly. "Hey! Focus. Who cured Lucky of a reptile dysfunction?" I demanded.

Alucard shrugged. "The little dude ate one of Starlight's edibles and *poof*."

Lucky nodded excitedly and did a little twirl. Then he reached his hand into his pocket and pulled out a fistful of golden discs. "I'm pretty sure its real gold," he said, and then he flung them up into the air like confetti. They fell hard and fast, sinking into the sand, confirming they really were metal.

"His scales," Alucard explained. "He sheds them like crazy."

Gunnar noticed my panic and held up a beefy, scarred hand. "Don't worry. It's not permanent or anything. He's basically a shifter." Lucky smiled brightly and started inspecting his hand. I saw his face start to flush crimson and I realized he was trying to force the change.

"Don't pop a testicle," Alucard advised.

Lucky's hand suddenly shifted into a golden-scaled claw and he let out a sharp breath at the strain. He lifted up his claw for everyone to see and I noticed Raphael staring at him in stunned disbelief. I realized, in that moment, that Raphael probably hadn't known about the whole golden dragon bit.

That Lucky had become the Fifth Divine.

Gunnar eyed Raphael curiously. "Is he here to be executed?" I held out my arm, barring Raphael from overreacting and smiting the werewolf. Raphael was too busy staring at Lucky to pay any attention to Gunnar, even if he was one of the Dread Four. Gunnar scratched his beard and frowned at me. "You two didn't come here from the Garden of Eden jump point," he said, pointing a thumb over his shoulder at the tent we had set up specifically for travelers. "That's the only way out of Kansas City…"

I stared at the assorted mess of Freaks before me and let out a frustrated breath. "Team meeting. Heaven's been overtaken, I kidnapped Raphael, and the Four Horsemen summoned me to a hearing," I told them. "I declined to attend." I motioned for them to follow me into the mess tent, and then I physically tugged Raphael after me because he'd finally noticed the black sandnado behind us.

"What in the Heavens is that?" Raphael sputtered, pointing at the anomaly.

I tugged him harder, forcing him to trip over his own feet or follow me. "You'll find out soon enough, Raphael. It's why I brought you here." I shoved him into the mess tent ahead of me and then I turned to face Starlight's tent. "Put your Ewok back in your pants, Starlight!" I shouted. "We have business to discuss!"

I heard metal platters crashing to the ground inside his makeshift sex dungeon, followed by splashing sounds and more giggling. "But the mama bear is juuuuuust right!" he crowed back. Alucard burst out laughing and I let out a resigned sigh.

"Welcome to Team Dracula," I told Raphael as I entered the tent alongside Gunnar and Alucard.

"We have very warm beer," Gunnar suggested with a dry smirk as he lifted a dented can to his mouth. He took a long, exaggerated sip while staring Raphael in the eyes. "Ahhh," he murmured, licking his lips.

Alucard lifted a dusty plastic water bottle in cheers. "And tepid Holy Water that a moderately reliable priest blessed for us," he drawled before taking a drink.

Raphael didn't look impressed.

❧ 19 ❧

The three men and the teddy bear stared at me, looking like their souls were constipated.

Starlight exhaled a thick cloud of noxious smoke and my mouth dropped open to realize he'd been holding in the peyote smoke for over a minute. He leaned back in his seat with a dazed and confused expression, and I wasn't sure if it was his drugs or my retelling of recent events.

"Did she really bite your ass?" Alucard asked, scratching his head. I scowled at him and he shrugged.

"The Pearly Gates have been breached?" Gunnar asked.

Raphael hung his chin. "Destroyed is more accurate."

Alucard rose from the table and started pacing back and forth in the dusty tent. "I want to hear more about Satan's asshole. You said you saw dead nephilim alongside angels and demons?" The nephilim cuffs sat on the table in front of me as proof. I arched an eyebrow at Raphael who nodded his agreement. "Does that mean the nephilim helped destroy the gates or were they trying to protect them?"

I shrugged. "The only corpse we could accurately identify had both bracelets," I said. "Not one of mine."

Gunnar folded his beefy arms and let out a long breath. "Shit." He shot me a familiar look and opened his mouth, but I cut him off.

"We're not calling Nate, Gunnar. We would spend more time trying to catch him up to speed, wasting valuable time we obviously don't have. Besides, our Horsemen Masks are worthless against Heaven and Hell. I know he's powerful and has powerful allies, but we don't even know who our enemies are: Heaven, Hell, or the Vatican. Are we against one or all three?"

"Kill them all and let God sort them out," Alucard murmured darkly. "No offense, Raphael."

Before Raphael could react, I leaned forward with a stern look. "God wasn't home, remember?" He winced and gave me a faint nod.

Gunnar let out a frustrated breath. "The Dread Four should work together, but you're right. The masks won't help here. And bringing in other pantheons is only going to make the war more confusing—"

"You bring Nate Temple here and the Apocalypse—or something much, *much* worse—starts now," Raphael said in a surprisingly concerned tone.

Starlight arched an eyebrow and then giggled nervously. The fact that it was a slightly frightened sound was what truly terrified me. Starlight was incredibly wise and mysterious, but I wasn't sure I had ever seen or heard him act nervously. Aloof and unconcerned or dismissive, yes. Scared?

No.

I frowned at Raphael. "What do you mean? Because it would bring the Dread Four together? Because it sure seems like the Apocalypse has already started, judging by what we saw at the Pearly Gates."

He shook his head firmly. "It has nothing to do with your masks. The only thing they can do here is get broken. Only the Four Horsemen have the ability to shut down the Sins."

"Or Archangels," Alucard reminded us.

Then Starlight slowly lifted his paw to point a claw at me. "Callie Penrose has made a habit of shutting down the Sins and Archangels. All by herself." He turned to Raphael with a curious look. "Because she is a Catalyst like Nate Temple? Or because she is a Master? Or is it something else?"

Raphael pursed his lips, actually seeming frustrated, like he was trying to claw the answer out of his own mind. It reminded me of those times when you're trying to remember a specific word but it keeps eluding you, perched right on the tip of your tongue but impossible to voice.

He finally leaned forward and met each of our eyes individually. "Whatever Calvin and Makayla Temple did with you three children was done out of sight, yet every single pantheon and higher power felt the repercussions." Starlight nodded his agreement, not seeming to realize he was doing it.

"When you three babies cried for the first time, the world felt ripples of power slam into everything we thought we once knew, cracking the foundations of our dynasties. It. Shook. Our. Faith." He leaned back in his chair and snatched a warm beer from the cooler. He cracked it open and guzzled the entire thing like he was kicking off happy hour after work. "Everything we were so confident in—that God had a plan and that we were all working for his Divine Will—fractured, and long-time friends and confidantes became risks. Everyone felt it. That was the cry heard around the world," he said, turning to face me directly. "That was the start of the war to end all wars, and Our Father never told us a damned thing about it. It destroyed us. Broke us. The Cherubim and Seraphim went rogue, slaughtering anyone and anything with wings, believing we in Heaven had caused the disturbance. We eventually locked them up, but not before hundreds of angels lay dead in the streets of Paradise."

I felt everyone staring at me but I pretended not to notice. "That...seems a little exaggerated, Raphael."

He snorted and shook his head. "We didn't know what to do, and your parents had concealed each of you in different ways. A war we had never heard of had begun yet we had no enemies in sight." His eyes grew distant and he was silent for about ten seconds. "Without answers or explanations from the present or future, we dusted off our history books to focus on the past," he said, sounding sick to his stomach. "We dispatched teams of angels to hunt babies on Earth," he whispered. "We kidnapped children in search of the threat. Some teams even murdered those children in search of you three."

Gunnar jumped to his feet with a furious growl and I saw fur rise up from his forearms as his hands shifted to claws. He lunged for Raphael with a murderous gleam in his eye. Starlight grabbed him with a surprisingly delicate grip and Gunnar dropped to his knees with a startled yelp of pain. Pressure points were fun.

Raphael didn't even move. In fact, he looked as if he would have welcomed Gunnar's punishment to fill the regret consuming him from within.

I stared at the Archangel in disgust and horror. "You...killed children?" I whispered. "To find me, Nate, and Quinn?"

He nodded ever so faintly, his gaze still a million miles away. "Why do you think so many people go missing every year? When our kidnappings turned up fruitless, our panic grew exponentially until we were abducting anyone and everyone. A hint or whisper of a connection was enough for us. God was no longer there to advise us and we panicked. Fear became our steadfast faith, and I'm not just talking about the angels in Heaven. Hell did it too. So did the other pantheons. Everyone was terrified. Gods and Titans fled their kingdoms, turning on each other or turning their backs on the world. Order collapsed and pandemonium rampaged. God was not dead. He was usurped by panic."

I felt like I wanted to vomit. How had I never heard this? Did Nate know any of this? Gunnar awkwardly climbed back into his chair but he was glaring at Raphael with murderous intent.

Alucard studied the Archangel with a troubled expression on his face. "You started making allies with your longtime enemies," he said softly, teasing out his own thoughts to gauge the archangel's reaction.

Raphael lowered his eyes in shame and gave a weak nod. "Y-yes."

Alucard propped his elbows on the table and leaned towards Raphael. "You...teamed up with demons and other gods, pooling your resources to see if anyone knew something you didn't. You were so terrified of these three babies—at the power they might one day take from you—that you forgave eons of crimes and betrayals to work together. You circled the wagons."

"May God forgive us," Raphael croaked.

"It looks like your Father went to the gas station for a pack of smokes and a lottery ticket and never came home, pal," Alucard said. "You get used to it once you learn that life isn't fair."

I frowned, dismissing the pessimistic vampire. "That's why Heaven and Hell don't seem particularly interested in policing each other. You...are fucking allies in this secret war!" I exclaimed.

Raphael grimaced and ultimately shook his head. "Not allies. It would be more accurate to say that we adopted the wartime philosophy that the enemy of my enemy is my friend."

Alucard snorted and shook his head in disgust. "More like the ends justifies the means."

I pondered this startling development, connecting what felt like a billion dots from the past—all the contradictions that suddenly made more sense. None of the other pantheons were friends, necessarily, but they all belonged to the same tribe. They were lower-case gods—rulers in charge of the rabble—and they sensed a peasant uprising on the wind. Not wanting to lose their positions of power, they had banded together behind the scenes to form a unified front against humanity.

"You lost control, though, didn't you?" I asked, realizing that I was smiling. "You convinced yourselves that it was acceptable to temporarily suspend your morals to achieve what you saw as a common goal. You cracked the foundation of your kingdom in order to make your defensive walls taller and thicker, not realizing the fatal flaw. You partnered with potential enemies who harbor the same fears but not necessarily the same goals. Your cure was worse than the disease, and now you expect us to give you pity for your troubles? To accept your tears of regret as recompense for your oh so noble intentions?" I shook my head in disbelief. "The mere thought that you might lose your stranglehold on power caused you to self-implode. Talk about not being worthy of your inheritance!" I snapped, cracking my words like a whip. "The ultimate throne of narcissism is when you cannibalize yourself so that no one else has the chance to eat your leg."

Alucard nodded. "You seppuku'd yourselves rather than facing the shame of potential defeat."

Gunnar studied me and then Alucard with a harsh look. "They. Killed. Children," he growled. "I don't give a fuck whether they did it because they were narcissists or because the Flying Spaghetti Monster told them to. They deserve to be thrown into a pit with enough food to last them an eternity so that they may rot in the well of their own shit and piss, unable to ignore the consequences of their actions."

Raphael curled a lip at Gunnar in an act of reflexive self-defense, but it almost immediately shattered into self-loathing and shame. "We were afraid!" he croaked. "How do you defeat an intangible fear?"

I stared him in the eyes and sneered. "You get *braver*. Fear doesn't ever die, archangel, bravery simply hits puberty and throat-punches all the beta cowards whining about their feelings. Or it dies trying."

The resulting silence was as sharp as a knife. "I don't seek your pity. I am not asking for your forgiveness—"

"Well, you're sure as shit not getting any absolution," Alucard yelled as he slammed his Horseman's Mask on the table hard enough for the legs to wobble and creak. The Mask of Absolution seemed to sneer at the Archangel.

Raphael again bowed his head meekly. "I am trying to help," he said softly. "I know what we did was wrong, but you are incorrectly placing all the blame on my shoulders. You are missing the fact that everyone agreed upon this course of action. Fae, Norse, Greek, Heaven and Hell..." he waggled a hand in a gesture that implied everyone else.

I frowned as I digested his words. "The Four Horsemen..." I mused. "What did they think of your little ploy?" I asked, wondering if this answered the question on why they seemed so incompetent at managing Heaven and Hell.

Raphael shrugged. "They seemed to agree with the plan," he admitted. "They never spoke of it, but they have always preferred their independence and don't typically let us know their thoughts. They simply act when they see fit, so I imagine they would have started slaughtering us if they disagreed."

I nodded absently, not knowing if I bought it entirely. They definitely hadn't stopped the cancerous tactics of the terrified gods and demons and angels, but they hadn't necessarily helped them either. Or...had they? Death had shown an affinity for Nate Temple over the past few years, even risking some sort of cosmic balance to help Nate reunite with Kára in what seemed like a cheap rom-com bodysnatcher story arc. That was the opposite of helping the pantheons.

"But if you knew it was all related to Nate's parents setting up Nate, me, and Quinn as quasi-Catalysts, why didn't everyone simply unite to take us down?" I asked.

Raphael pursed his lips. "Calvin and Makayla Temple got themselves killed before anyone started looking too closely at you three. In fact, all of your scheming parents seemed to die before they could be questioned. And they died in ways that prevented anyone from interrogating them. Simply put, we had no idea who was behind it until recent years, but by then you three were too powerful to easily dismiss. Factions from our original coalition had apparently started making deals with you three, drawing new battle lines that were not so easily crossed," Raphael said. "Calvin and Makayla Temple laid many false trails to keep us busy. By the time our side had started questioning Freaks, we were soon confronted by a shadowy organization of Freaks and gods and heroes," he said with a frown.

I leaned forward. "You mean the Masters?" I asked.

He turned to me and gave a slow nod. "They did not immediately tell us their organization's name, but yes. Unfortunately, many of our allies had also made alliances with these Masters so that none of us knew exactly who was working with who. When anyone started digging too deep into the Masters they wound up dead or disappeared."

I nodded. "Well, we're against them and so are you, right?"

He blinked at me. "From what I gather, you are one of them. As is Nate Temple."

I scoffed. "I earned my membership card by mistake and Nate inherited his without any foreknowledge. Is Quinn MacKenna also a Master?"

He gave me a dubious frown, not seeming to believe my claim or the sincerity of my question—as if he thought I was setting him up for some kind of trap. "How should I know? Thankfully, she hasn't stuck her head into our realm. Ask the Fae or Norse what kind of insanity she's stirring up." He let out a frustrated sigh. "I no longer know where the lines are drawn. My own brother Michael made a deal with you and you turned him into an Anghellian and a Divine. The Vatican have added a second collar to the nephilim we assigned to them, but I don't know where that bracelet came from," he said, eyeing the black cuff on the table. "The Sins seem friendly with you and your team. I was betrayed by my brother Uriel, learning too late that he had his own thirst for power and that he wanted you dead. The nephilim have gone utterly rogue and no longer follow my orders, but I don't know if that has to do with Uriel's fall or those cursed black bracelets." He flung up his hands in frustration. "As far as I can tell, I am one of the very few looking to help you balance the scales or at least find out what is truly going on here—"

Lucky strolled into the tent with a bright grin and Raphael immediately cut off. "When are we going to try busting out Azazel and Samzaya again?"

Raphael stiffened like a board and his eyes practically bugged out of his scarred face. "The watchers?" he whispered in disbelief. Then his eyes tracked towards the tent's exit and understanding dawned on him. "The sandstorm. It is the prison Uriel created!" he hissed, rising to his feet. "I must speak to them!"

I mirrored his gesture and held out my palm in the universal *stop* gesture. "Wait, Raphael! It isn't safe to go near it, and we don't know how to get in yet!"

Raphael flared out his wings, knocking all of us back onto our asses. Lucky promptly shifted into his golden dragon form and tore through the side of the tent in a blast of fire. Raphael also bolted out the entrance like the devil was hot on his heels. "I am Archangel Raphael!" he shouted arrogantly. "I will break my way inside!"

I sat up with a curse, pushing one of the rickety folding chairs off my chest. Gunnar and Alucard had done the same, but Starlight was already back on his feet and staring out the tent's entrance with a pensive frown. He turned to look at me and shrugged mischievously. "Well, we no longer need a semi-human guinea pig," he said with an amused chuckle. "Let's go watch how quickly archangel armor gets destroyed." Then he promptly strolled out of the tent, motioning for us to follow.

I saw the nephilim cuffs in the rubble and scooped them up. Then I shoved them inside my satchel, jumped to my feet, and started running. Gunnar and Alucard were hot on my heels.

✵ 21 ✵

Starlight plopped himself down on the ground to watch from under the shade of the camouflage canopy.

I sprinted towards the ominous, entirely unnatural sandstorm with a severe sense of trepidation in my chest. Gunnar growled as he and Alucard caught up with me. Raphael screamed across the desert, hovering just above the ground as he flapped his wings for more speed.

The watchers' prison loomed ahead.

It wasn't truly a sandstorm in any scientific sense of the term, but we'd taken to calling it that for the sake of maintaining our sanity. Unlike typical tornadoes where the tip touched the ground and the tornado grew wider as it stretched up into the sky, this phenomenon looked more like a pyramid made of rapidly swirling black diamond grit.

Sparks and embers whipped through the screaming wind, reminding me of my brief visit to Purgatory or when I had crossed Samael's bridge to Castle Dracula for our very first godfather-daughter-date. That seemed like years ago.

But looking into this haunting void of the Neverwas felt just as chilling as the other two times. I wondered if the black grit was actually an army of wayward souls spiraling in a raging ring of death and destruction. In Purgatory and the Neverwas there had been no storms to compare to this. It was as if someone had shaken up the atmosphere of the Neverwas inside a snow globe and plopped it down here in the middle of the Sahara desert.

"Why did Lucky have to say their names?" I growled, pumping my arms as I ran after Raphael.

"Because Lucky is an asshole?" Alucard offered drily.

"We're not really going to let him try to get inside, are we?" Gunnar asked. "Every single camel we sent through was ripped to shreds on contact. Seventeen so far. I know archangels are strong, but I'm pretty sure this storm was specifically designed to keep archangels and Sins out, right?"

I nodded, trying not to remember the camels we had inadvertently slaughtered while trying to figure out how to get inside the dome. Seventeen? They must have tried a few more today while I was away. The Divines had been taking shifts throwing their combined powers at the sandstorm in order to try and weaken it or break it entirely. Lucky had watched them, not knowing how to do the beam of light thing they had done at the Garden of Eden. Looking at the storm now, it sure didn't look any weaker than the first time I'd seen it a few days ago. But I needed the nephilim on my side for the war, and the only way to get them all at once was to get these watchers freed from their prison.

Theoretically speaking, of course. I had to convince them—violently—to agree to help me.

Gunnar drew a pistol that looked big and heavy enough to put down a dinosaur. He thumbed back the hammer and lifted it high enough for me to see as he shot me an inquisitive look.

I gritted my teeth and considered the suggestion. Finally, I let out a frustrated shake of my head. "Not yet. Starlight is right. If Raphael wants to try going in, we'll learn whether the Divines really have managed to neutralize the dangers of entering," I said. "Which will mean we can go in after him." I hesitated. "Keep your gun cocked and loaded, Gunnar. I don't know what he intends for Azazel and Samzaya, but it will most likely not align with our interests. It likely won't align with the watchers' interests either," I added. "Raphael's brother is the one who imprisoned them in the first place."

He nodded and lowered the gun slightly.

"One problem, Callie," Alucard said, his eyes glittering with golden light as his body absorbed power from the broiling sun. "The Divines have already made two attempts today and I think they're recovering with a little siesta," he said, pointing at the temporary shelters we had set up at equidistant points around the perimeter of the sandstorm. Only two were within view from our current position. I saw Xuanwu's massive turtle feet poking out from within his tent and I realized that he was taking in some much-needed shade.

"Damn it!" I hissed, jerking my head to the opposite side just in time to see Zoe, the Vermillion Bird—a fiery phoenix, technically speaking, but it seemed rude to completely dismiss her official historic title—poke her head out from within her tent. She cocked her head at me in startled confusion and I waved my hands desperately as I pointed at the sandstorm and shouted, "IT'S MORPHIN TIME!"

Alucard laughed. "This is my favorite part." His smile faded. "As long as they don't die or burn themselves out, of course."

Zoe's tent exploded in flames and she let out a bone-chilling shriek that made me miss a step. Ahead of us, Raphael dropped down to the ground and drew a sword, except he was moving too fast to stop on a dime, so his feet hit the sand like an anchor and his body kept going forward until he head-butted the ground and flipped forward in a truly terrible-looking summersault. His wings flopped and flapped in an effort to slow him down, but they only served to cause him more trouble.

The archangel was a screaming tumbleweed of feathers and pride, but he passed the one-hundred-yard marker in his fall.

Xuanwu's tent exploded in a porcupine explosion of icicles and snow as the Black Tortoise let out a beastly roar. He lifted his sword cane as his eyes locked onto the tumbling archangel approaching the sandstorm, and his obsidian eyes glittered murderously. I flung up a pink fireball into the air and screamed at the top of my lungs while waving my hands at him. "IT'S MORPHIN TIME, XUANWU! STOP THE STORM! WARN BAI AND QINGLONG *NOW!!*" I roared. "WE NEED ALL OF YOU TO UNLEASH EVERYTHING YOU HAVE ON THAT STORM AS FAST AS YOU FUCKING CAN!" Then I started hurling more blasts of pink fireballs around the perimeter of the sandstorm, hoping to catch the attention of Qinglong and Bai who were on the opposite side of the sandstorm in their relative positions at the Cardinal directions of the compass.

Xuanwu abruptly disappeared and I let out a breath of relief. Xuanwu was impossibly fast, even though he looked like an arthritic, calcified snapping turtle whose catchphrase was *back in my day...* He held a sword he could never release and seemed to move slow as molasses, but when the situation called for it, he could move faster than absolutely everyone I had ever met.

Gunnar reached for his Mask but I grabbed his forearm firmly and shook my head. "No. You saw what happened to my Mask when I used it against Envy," I reminded him.

He curled his lip and nodded. Then he exploded into his Wulfric form, suddenly towering over us. Alucard shrugged and snapped his fingers dramatically. His eyes suddenly flared with golden light and his hands started dripping with molten lava. Apparently, his daywalker powers were maturing, because he hadn't needed his Mask to make lava.

I frowned and pursed my lips, realizing I didn't have any trendy transformation at hand. So I shrugged and summoned up Thunder and Terror, my fiery swords.

Alucard snickered and Gunnar huffed in amusement. "Easy there, Thoros of Myr," Alucard teased. I conked him on the head with the hilt of one of my swords and he grunted in surprise. Then he scowled. "You are a bad sport, Callie Penrose."

Gunnar held up his massive claws in an innocent gesture and I rolled my eyes as I let the swords wink out. I had no use for them at the moment, so it was kind of a silly gesture. "Raphael!" I bellowed as I resumed hurling pink flares into the sky to alert Bai and Qinglong. "It's suicide!" I screamed.

The archangel continued on, ignoring my warnings.

I ran as fast as possible, knowing that Raphael's plan was going to get him killed, and that if he died under my care—since everyone had watched me kidnap him against his will—no one would believe he'd gotten *himself* killed for being a moron. I would become Raphael's assassin.

One-by-one, beams of light screamed up into the sky as Bai and Qinglong got the message and combined their powers in an effort to destroy the black sandstorm of sorrow, much like they had done to unlock the Garden of Eden for me days before. I doubted they were ready for this surge of power.

But now it was time to toss out the rose petals, turn on some Marvin Gaye, and get ready to make some bad decisions, because date night was on, whether they were ready for it or not. Xuanwu reappeared in his spot and added his own beam of light to the mix until all four arced up over the sandstorm and converged together to try and break the prison open.

They melded together at the peak of the pyramid, and a deep gong reverberated throughout the desert as if we were in an enclosed auditorium. My sense of equilibrium wobbled and I blinked rapidly. I almost lost my footing as the sandstorm abruptly froze still, no longer twirling in a rapid vortex. Now, it was just a wall of glittering black flecks of sand interspersed with embers and sparks.

"What in the living hell?" I wheezed. "Why has that never happened before?" I demanded. Neither of my allies answered me. What was even more unnerving was the fact that it still didn't look...open. As if the sand was still an impenetrable and deadly wall. Just because it had stopped spinning didn't mean it was any less dangerous than before.

Perhaps it was even more dangerous now.

Raphael started running even faster, using his wings to increase his speed across the hot sand.

Not knowing what else to do, I started flinging fireballs directly at him in an effort to at least trip him up. His archangel armor shimmered into being in an instant, and my fireballs ricocheted off of him like water on a hot griddle. Gunnar let out a tremendous howl and started firing his horse pistol upon the archangel.

It did no good either. I used my wizard's magic to lift up a wall of sand directly before the archangel, and then I set it to spinning, creating two more of the whirling sandnadoes for him to contend with. Then I grabbed Gunnar and Alucard by the sleeve and Shadow Walked directly up to the barrier in front of Raphael, wondering why I hadn't thought of it earlier.

We appeared in front of the archangel with the deadly prison at our backs. Raphael was swinging his sword at the sandnadoes, spitting curses in a language I didn't understand, but it sounded harsh and guttural.

I looked up at the sky to see Lucky in his golden dragon form hovering overhead, shifting his attention from us to whatever the hell was going on at the peak of the now motionless sandstorm. He looked deeply troubled as he stared at the intersection of power forming an X over the tip of the pyramid.

"Do something, Lucky!" I yelled at the top of my lungs.

Raphael finally beat back the tempests of sand and stared us down with a determined scowl. "Stand down, White Rose. I would speak with my long lost brothers."

I pointed at the pile of camel carcasses a few dozen paces away. "It is suicide, Raphael! I'm not trying to stop you from speaking with them, I'm trying to prevent you from killing yourself. When we find a safe path inside,

I swear I will let you talk their ears off. Killing yourself won't prove anything, but it will make everything much, much worse."

He dismissed the camel carcasses with a pompous sneer and then studied me in silence. I couldn't tell what he was thinking. "You saw the Pearly Gates," he finally said. "There is no time for patience. This is the end, whether it is safe or not," he said, practically spitting at the word *safe* as if to call me a coward for daring to warn him, an archangel of the Lord.

Stupid men. Everything was always a challenge to their honor. "What good will it do the Pearly Gates situation if you run into a meat grinder and turn into a thousand scraps of flesh and bone?" I shouted, pointing my thumb behind me at the now eerily motionless wall of black sand.

Raphael puffed up his chest proudly. "I am Archangel Raphael. I demand that you stand down and let me pass. I will not be responsible for the consequences of you barring my path." He sneered openly at Gunnar and Alucard. "The Dread Four hold no power over Heaven."

Gunnar's lips curled back into a hungry grin, revealing massive fangs. "I don't need a mask to chew on a talking bag of bones," he growled, tossing his pistol to the side and extending his claws.

Alucard smiled wickedly as he lifted his molten lava hands. "I smell fried chicken, Gunnar," he drawled.

I held out my hands for everyone to dial it down. I opened my mouth but Lucky's cry abruptly cut me off.

"To infinity! And beyond!" he roared, spitting out a beam of liquid fire at the peak of the black pyramid. Everyone craned their neck to stare up at the golden dragon in disbelief.

A horrifying, shattering sound cracked through the landscape, sounding like breaking glass, and then a jagged opening ripped down from the top of the wall of sand like a glacier calving. No, it *was* a lightning bolt! It slammed into the ground directly behind me, sending the Dread Four cartwheeling through the air.

✢ 2 2 ✢

I landed on a mound of hot sand a dozen paces away, and I heard
Gunnar and Alucard slam into each other just below me. Thankfully,
we hadn't knocked each other out.

"Motherlucking fucky!" Alucard cursed. "Get off me, you filthy animal,"
he complained at Gunnar, who was sprawled out atop him and blinking up at
the sky with a startled expression on his face. Maybe the bolt of lightning
had singed his tail.

I jerked my attention back to the wall of sand to see Raphael crouched
down on one knee and using his wing like a Spartan shield directly in front
of him. He was clenching his teeth as sand blasted around him, fighting to
push him back, but he withstood the force with sheer stubbornness. It died
down a moment later and he peered over his wing to see a jagged rift now
splitting the wall of motionless sand.

A path through the chaos.

Like Moses parting the Red Sea.

Shit. Had Lucky done it? Or had he just made everything infinitely
worse? This was what we had wanted, after all—a way inside. Raphael rose to
his feet and his wings disappeared from view. He glanced over his shoulder
and met my eyes with a victorious smile. Then he sprinted into the divide.

Before I could even react, I felt a mental presence hit me like a slap in
the face.

M-Master! Sanguina shouted, making my brain vibrate in an uncomfortable way. And I suddenly felt her proximity within the sandstorm. She was alive and well, but she seemed severely weakened. This was the first time I'd had direct contact with her in recent weeks, and I let out a breath of relief to hear she was safe.

"I'm coming!" I shouted at her as I climbed to my feet and started running towards the rift, not even waiting for Gunnar and Alucard to join me.

N-no! she snapped, stuttering strangely. *N-not yet! They will k-kill any intruder. G-give me more time!*

I almost lost my footing, but I caught myself just in time. "Bad news, Sanguina. Archangel Raphael really, *really* wants to speak with them, and he won't take no for an answer. He's on his way right now," I snapped. "And I'm right behind him."

Her reply was a horrified silence, and I knew things had just gotten a helluva lot worse for me. I raced into the rift and shuddered as the darkness surrounding me seemed to swallow me up. The path zigzagged left and right like we were in the depths of some massive crevice in the bowels of a forgotten mountain range. The motionless sand on either side of me was haunting, making me feel like I was underwater. The sun didn't pierce the murky depths of the rift, even though I could see a thin point of sky high overhead—the peak of the pyramid. The temperature dropped by about fifty degrees and my fingers started to feel numb like I had frostbite. Each step felt like I was running across a frozen pond, and the ground was fracturing deep beneath me, the fissures spiderwebbing out across the desert.

The silence was what really messed with my head, though. I couldn't hear Raphael ahead of me and I couldn't hear my allies behind me.

But I heard one thing very clearly.

Then R-Raphael shall d-die, Sanguina's voice stammered in a matter-of-fact tone.

I tried to ignore the painful burn on my lips; they felt chapped and raw, cracking at even the slightest movement. I looked down to see that the tips of my fingers were turning purple and that I could no longer feel them. Vapor escaped my lips, but the moisture only served to freeze before my eyes and hit my skin like a sandblaster. I stumbled and almost tripped as my leg started to give out on me; not being able to feel my toes through the arctic cold was making it almost impossible to rely on my feet for stability.

Without consciously realizing it, I drew my fiery swords from within my soul and I felt an immediate wave of heat rip through my body, hitting the tips of my fingers and toes like thin bamboo reeds driven beneath my fingernails. I cried out and convulsed violently as the heat rocked through me, burning away the frigid cold that had been on the verge of overwhelming me. If the swords hadn't been part of my very soul, my numb hands would have likely fumbled them, but I held tight and they burned bright.

Thunder and Terror were extensions of my willpower, symbolizing my parents' sacrifice and love.

Water dripped from the walls of sand and I realized that it was actually frozen solid even though it was made of air and grit. My chest grew looser as the arctic temperature lost its grip on me. I let out a breath of relief, suddenly realizing why Uriel had needed the fiery sword to confront Azazel and Samzaya.

Why Sanguina had been stammering and stuttering. She was quite literally freezing. The temperature had almost knocked me down within moments, and she had been inside the storm for...days, possibly weeks.

How the living hell had this prison of ice been formed in the middle of a desert? I wasn't sure I had ever felt anything so cold. It had been so extreme that my body hadn't even been able to process the danger until the consequences of my exposure were impossible to ignore: numb and blackened fingers, splitting and chafing lips, raw, frost burned cheeks.

I shook my head and tested my feet by placing pressure on them. Pins and needles shot through my toes and I heard more of the thunderous cracks deep within the sandy earth, but my feet could now support me again. I called back, remembering Gunnar and Alucard. "Stay out of here! It's magically warded with some kind of arctic spell that will freeze you to death! Only women are strong enough to handle it!" I smirked faintly, knowing how angry that comment would make them. Might as well twist the knife. "We all know how lethal common colds are to the common man."

I heard stammering and muttering from a few twists back behind me as the two bickered while trying not to freeze to death. They knew about my fiery swords, so they were probably using that fact to justify their agreement with my reprimand. "F-fine!" Alucard drawled, sounding sleepy. "Five m-minutes and I s-start hurling l-lava into this f-f-f-f—" His stammering abruptly cut off, followed by a frustrated sound. "F-fucking fro-asis."

Gunnar snarled in frustration and I heard him either stomp his massive paw or punch the frozen wall of sand. I couldn't see them, so I had no idea which, but I sure felt it. Whatever his violent outburst had been, it made the entire cavern of mystery shudder, groan, and emit an alarming string of popping, cracking, and hissing shrieks.

"What the fuck, Gunnar?!" I demanded. "Bad dog! Git!"

Alucard laughed weakly and I heard Gunnar let out an apologetic whine before Alucard's stammering, reassuring voice guided the pair back towards the entrance. I let out a sigh of relief, spun on my heels, and then I latched onto my bond with Sanguina, using her as a compass. Then I started running as fast as I possibly could, holding my fiery swords out before me like torches.

Thunder and Terror heralded the Horseman of Despair as she plunged deeper into the frozen desert oasis—the fro-asis, as Alucard had dubbed it.

The daywalker vampire might have been able to light himself on fire to withstand the cold, but what if that served to completely shatter the ground beneath us? His lava hands hadn't seemed to protect him from the cold in the first place. And Gunnar was massive—his weight on the fragile ground could definitely send us plummeting to our...

Well, whatever end awaited us beneath the frozen sand. Was I really standing atop some kind of frozen lake? Had the impossible black sandstorm been concealing it from view?

I studied the walls to either side, wondering what the Four Divines had done differently to make the sandstorm finally stop spinning. I had absolutely no idea how Lucky had finally figured out what to do—desperation, perhaps—but he'd opened the tunnel into this madness, and now I was on my own. But if it had taken all five of the Divines to unlock the prison, how had Uriel intended to get back in here to kill Azazel and Samzaya? I'd already tried the most basic idea of walking up to the sandstorm with my fiery swords and poking it.

It had done absolutely nothing other than causing my swords to emit a shower of sparks and molten black sand to fall down upon my face and head, forcing me to run away screaming and swatting at my hair and shoulders. The skin over my knuckles had been so burned and blistered that Aala had forced me to take a dip in the healing pond at Xuanwu's estate.

So, how had Sanguina entered without stopping the sand? Every living creature we'd tried sending into the storm had been shredded down to the bones within seconds—dying so quickly that the camels hadn't even had time to scream. I'd tried sending my butterflays into the storm and they'd been flung back out like ricocheting bullets.

As far as I knew, Xuanwu and his siblings hadn't done anything they hadn't tried a dozen times already. Had they simply worn it down enough that it had finally worked? Kind of like when you tried opening a jar of pickles for ten minutes only to give up and hand it to a buddy who twisted it open on their first try with no apparent effort. Your ten minutes of anger had loosened it up just enough to open on the next try.

Maybe today had been the culmination of the pickle jar lid finally loosening up enough to share its pickley love with the world for the first time.

I dismissed it as irrelevant, devoting my full attention to the current moment rather than the *how* question. Raphael was on a suicide mission, and that was really going to tarnish my already threadbare reputation with Heaven. Everyone had seen me kidnap him—after ducking out on a hearing with the Four Horsemen—and if Raphael got himself killed, I would look guilty as...

Sin.

But it was far worse than that. If Raphael died, absolutely no one would believe me when I brought them the news about the Pearly Gates being assaulted. I didn't even know how to get back up there. Raphael had looked so surprised at finding himself outside the Pearly Gates that I was betting we'd crashed through an entrance that shouldn't have been crashable. Technically, we'd appeared in the area where dead souls would arrive to be judged.

It was plausible that Raphael had never even set foot there before. The *I just shit my Holy robe*s look I had seen on his face seemed like irrefutable evidence of that fact.

I didn't even want to consider the secondary and tertiary consequences I would suffer if Raphael got himself killed by the watchers. For one, the remaining archangels and Sins, and probably the Four Horsemen would immediately want to execute the two watchers, which would ruin my chances at taking back the nephilim.

I either needed to save Raphael or find a way to break the watchers free of their chains and bind them to my cause in the next five minutes. None of those options seemed like they had good odds of success since I still had no idea who had assaulted the Pearly Gates, or what Gabriel and Wrath really wanted with all of this chaos.

I knew Wrath had wanted me to become his bride at one point, but that plan had failed. Other than the strange dark prophecy he had shared, I had no idea why it had been so important to him or what it had to do with Gabriel.

I didn't even know where the two douchebags were at present.

23

I kept my eyes on the walls as I ran because I entertained the sudden fear that perhaps a bunch of somethings were living inside the darkness. I found myself envisioning thousands of angelic mummies lifting their arms towards me and shambling forward in a mindless, never-ending, moaning mass of soiled linens.

I even started to see silhouettes in the depths of the black sand that I could have sworn were enemies or glowing eyes, even though they were likely just frozen embers and imagined forms. A sharp, splintering *rat-a-tat* cracking sound beneath my feet caused me to let out a nervous gasp as I felt the ground shudder and groan. Had I imagined it rippling beneath me in a rolling motion?

I pressed on, hoping that Raphael wasn't too far ahead of me—or already dead—because I could sense Sanguina nearby. The entire rift had been dark, but as I drew closer to Sanguina, the shadowy gloom seemed to grow thicker —almost a physical substance, like I could stick my tongue out and lick up some of the darkness.

I rounded the last corner and entered a dark, foggy, circular chamber with no other exits. I almost skidded directly into Raphael since he was standing in front of me without making a sound. His wings suddenly flared out with a strange crackling sound, and he hopped laterally to get out of my way. I tried to stop but I kept right on sliding into the enclosure, holding my fiery swords out to the side as if they could halt my forward progress.

Out of the thick mist, a snarling face suddenly loomed before me, lashing out with bright white fangs. I reared my head back as far as possible, and the teeth snapped closed hard enough to create a loud, echoing, clacking sound as they just barely avoided ripping my throat out. I pivoted and backhanded the face with the hilt of one of my fiery swords sending out a shower of sparks as the feral monster disappeared back out of sight. Thankfully, the force of my blow had been enough to stop my sliding advance, and I was back in control of my feet. I panted desperately as I kept my head on a swivel and the swords out in front of me. A harsh, hoarse chuckle reverberated off the walls and swarmed around me like a cave of disturbed bats as I cautiously backed up a few steps.

I heard a clinking metallic scrape in the darkness, and then I felt a great blast of air that knocked me on my ass and sent me sliding back. Raphael caught me and pulled me to my feet, but he never actually peeled his eyes away from the obvious threat to assess me for injuries.

"We're leaving," I growled, reaching out to grab him by the wrist.

Except he yanked his hand clear before I could make contact. "No. I w-will have answers from the t-traitors," he stammered with surprising conviction. He was holding his sword out before him and I noticed that his archangel armor was covered in frost and icicles. Even his wings were sluggish and frozen in places. His eyebrows were dusted with snow, and his scarred face sported a few black and red spots from the frostbite. My eyes widened in surprise. It was cold enough to freeze an archangel?

A dark, malevolent laugh echoed out from the impenetrable mist before us. "You hear that, Azazel? Raph believes the rumors. Thinks we've been bad little boys." The cold, sinister voice laughed harder, and I found myself lifting my fiery swords towards the sound on instinct. Samzaya's laugh made me feel like a cat with its fur rubbed the wrong way, but maybe that was just because he'd tried to eat me.

"Gabriel's lapdog," the other voice replied in a dismissive, condescending tone. "You won't last much longer down here, brother. Be gone!" The second voice—Azazel—was calm and stoic. He sounded cruel and just, unwavering and determined. Resolute in his convictions, and unsympathetic to fragility of any kind whatsoever, even if it stemmed from mercy.

"Sanguina?" I demanded. "An introduction would be swell. If they continue measuring their peckers, I'm going to start plucking all three of them and then let God sort them out."

There was a stunned silence in the misty space. Even Raphael shot me a stunned, disgusted look.

Sanguina sent me a mental embrace that was the equivalent of a full-bodied hug. "Gentlemen, may I introduce you to Callie Penrose, daughter of Nephilim Titus and Constance Solomon. Master Dracula and Horsewoman of Despair." Her voice boomed into the cavern like a living entity of its own, and I found myself smiling. "She's the one wielding Thunder and Terror, so I assume that means..." She trailed off and I realized she was setting me up to spike the figurative volleyball on these clowns.

I took a bold step forward, extended my fiery swords to the side and then I took a royal bow. "I killed Uriel and took his armor. I wield Thunder and Terror, I guard the Garden of Eden, and I bonded with Envy's Halo—"

Azazel and Samzaya interrupted me with furious, animalistic snarls from within the mist and their chains creaked and groaned as the two watchers rushed me in unison. Raphael yanked me back behind him with a sluggish motion and lifted his sword as he placed his body directly between me and the psychotic watchers. For the second time, I fell on my ass and slid, but this time I bumped into the wall with a grunt. I stared at Raphael's back with wide, panicked eyes as two massive black specters took shape in the mist. I couldn't see the actual watchers, just their nightmarish silhouettes. They looked like shadow monsters of claws and fangs.

They pounced upon Raphael and ripped him limb-from-limb, tearing away his armor like it was seafood night, and the archangel's shell was the only thing standing between them and happiness. Raphael's sword shattered like brittle glass and the archangel went down with a gurgled, choking gasp, and the sounds of ripping flesh.

Sanguina bounded into my lap and placed her paws on my chest so that she was head-level with me and blocking me from witnessing any more of the watchers' archangel feast. "Flee, Callie! I warned you. They were not ready for visitors yet. Perhaps not ever again, but certainly not now!"

I stared at her woodenly, realizing I was nodding numbly. "O-okay," I stammered.

Sanguina snarled and nipped my ear hard enough for me to cry out and leap to my feet. "GO!" She snarled, lunging for my ankles as if to bite me again.

I hopped back and the sounds of feasting abruptly stopped. The shadow monsters disappeared and silence reigned all around me. The smell of blood was thick in the air and I almost gagged at the memory of tasting Raphael's blood earlier.

I was nothing like them, though. I was different.

Right?

A dark shape lunged towards me out of the mist and I instinctively swung both swords at it. A pair of emaciated, pale arms burst out of the mist and two clawed hands caught my fiery swords like they were nothing more than sticks swung by a toddler.

A haunting, pale-faced vampire with long, ivory fangs leaned out of the mist to stare directly at me. His eyes glowed solid red and he licked his lips hungrily, not even seeming to notice my fiery swords burning his palms and fingers. "Solomon..." he mused in a surprisingly seductive, honeyed tone. "It sounds like a rare dessert wine from my misspent youth."

I tried firing back a retort but I couldn't seem to make my mouth work. I was both horrified and awed at Samzaya's strength and his masterful ability to mesmerize me. I watched as his face appeared to grow healthier, already processing Raphael's blood to restore some of his natural looks after eons of imprisonment and starvation. He was vampire-gazing me right now and I couldn't help but appreciate the level of skill, like I was watching it happen to somebody else. I no longer had any doubts about the origin of the vampires.

This was him. Samzaya.

Sanguina was just a pale imitation.

"G-get back," I whispered, sensing his brother Azazel rising up from the mist beside Samzaya. I didn't dare look into his eyes, knowing I stood no chance of standing up to both of them at the same time.

Samzaya chuckled in amusement. Then he twisted his wrists and the fiery swords shattered into dozens of fragments. They fell to the ground like scattered coals, sending up trails of steam as they melted the frozen sand below.

I stared in horror at my now empty hands. Even the hilts had turned to dust. But...they were a part of me. Had he just obliterated a part of my soul?

Samzaya leered at me, amused by the stunned look on my face. "Ashes to ashes, dust to dust, Samzaya and Azazel will do as they must." Sanguina started yapping at him and he glanced down with a frown to find her at his feet, glaring at him with her one remaining eye. He sighed and took a step back from me. Then he gave me a formal bow. "It was such a pleasure meeting you, Callie. Dinner's calling me, and it's been so long since I've had a good meal," he said with a wicked grin. "Until next time."

Then he calmly turned away and strolled back into the fog.

I felt Azazel studying me in silence, but I couldn't make myself meet his gaze, unable to fathom what beautiful horrors I might find in Samzaya's brother, Envy's lover. I did notice him staring at the black ring on my finger —Envy's Halo.

"Are you the Dark Horse?" he asked, sounding both amused and suspicious at the same time.

It tickled something at the edge of my memory, but I was feeling lightheaded as the effects of Samzaya's gaze slowly began to wear off. "I...I thought you could help...but y-you're just monsters," I mumbled, taking a step back.

Azazel smiled in my peripheral vision and I thought I saw his eyes shimmer with a silver glow. "You are entirely, unequivocally correct, Callie Penrose," he said in a bold, surprisingly gentle tone that hinted at a much deeper meaning than his words suggested. "We are virtuous men—monsters who consciously *choose* when to act monstrously. We do not apologize for it. Non serviam, daughter of Solomon."

Then he winked at me and turned away, joining his brother in the frigid mist. Now that my fiery swords were destroyed, the cold started seeping back into my bones and I shuddered involuntarily. Sanguina nudged my ankles adamantly and dropped something into my hand. I clutched it tightly in my fist, too shaken to look at it. "Go before you freeze to death. They won't hesitate to eat you if you fall dead here. Go."

And with that helpful little visual, I shambled out of the sandstorm with abandon, no longer caring about the sounds of cracking ice all around me. My vision started to tunnel but I didn't dare slow down, even as it became obvious I was on the verge of blacking out. I felt tears spilling out from my eyes, but they froze almost the instant they spilled down my cheeks. I kept running, no longer feeling my fingers or toes.

I had failed. Lost. Doomed Kansas City.

My parents' legacy—Thunder and Terror—were forever lost. The fiery swords were extinguished.

Archangel Raphael was dead.

The Pearly Gates had been assaulted and I couldn't think of a way to tell anyone without incriminating myself, especially now with Raphael gone.

🦁 24 🦁

I woke up to the sounds of grown men singing and splashing water nearby. I felt a breeze dance across my skin and my flesh pebbled instinctively, even though it was balmy and pleasant. My eyes shot open as I processed the fact that my gooseflesh was on my breasts rather than my forearms. I glanced down to see that I was topless and wearing only a familiar white sarong around my hips.

I groaned and sat up, realizing exactly where I was. I squinted at the sunlight and shielded my eyes to assess my immediate surroundings. Demonic inmates who looked very much like Chippendale eye-candy were jumping off a diving board to perform seemingly impossible acrobatic maneuvers before splashing into a crystal blue pool. A gaggle of beautiful topless women held stacks of cards on their laps and chittered back and forth amongst themselves before shuffling through their cards and lifting one high above their heads with a number written on it. They were scoring the dives. They were also drinking heavily, but I was fairly certain the men were too, judging by the next contestant's attempt at a...triple backflip.

He hit the water back-first with a meaty slap and everyone winced and groaned in sympathy or pointed and laughed jovially.

No one took anything personally, and they were soon all drinking and laughing again. Tall marble columns surrounded the pool, and elegant fountains with beautiful statues dotted the little oasis of rolling, grassy hills. A pop-up bar near the pool was full of more topless people, and they all had similar blue and red glowing tattoos on their backs.

Demons, not people. Powerful, deadly, murdering...reformed demons.

All in all, it looked like utopia—naked people of pretty much all colors and sizes getting drunk, having fun, and genuinely not caring about anything other than living in the moment.

Of course, this was Solomon's Prison, and they had all been here for hundreds of years. This strange realm prevented all physical violence, and even cursing in anger was discouraged, because your tirade would be magically silenced and you would wind up projectile vomiting bubbles.

I climbed to my feet, ignoring the three people having sex a few feet away from me. The man was dutifully trying to satisfy two women, but he was obviously outnumbered and they had deep appetites. He looked like he fully intended to throw his back out or die trying and the women looked happy to oblige him.

They had an audience with scorecards as well. I turned away and pretended I hadn't seen anything.

This wasn't utopia. No one had any responsibilities whatsoever, and they were only permitted to live this way by the grace of my ancestor, King Solomon, who had designed the parameters for their carefree, eternal prison sentence. No one had to make food—let alone find food—and the alcohol never stopped flowing.

In the real world, someone had to gather and make those things for the revelers, so I wasn't naive enough to think any world could actually work this way. There would always be haves and have-nots. Workers and lazy bums.

But...

It was nice to pretend it was all real rather than one of the most amazingly cruel punishments—and accomplishments—imaginable. Solomon had turned some of the worst demons in the world to happy-go-lucky party animals with nary a mean-streak in sight. If I'd taken the time to scan the rap-sheets of even a handful of these beautiful naked people, I likely wouldn't have been able to sleep without nightmares for a week. This was all a facade.

"White Rose!" a handful of demons cheered, thankfully respecting my obvious desire for privacy. Maybe it was my frown, but they were wise enough not to approach.

I made my way towards the colossal recreation of Solomon's Temple and stared up towards the peak, which reached into the actual clouds. Not wanting to risk tripping into a conversation with any passersby, I summoned my angel wings and flew up into the sky. I flew fast and high, reveling in the speed and grace of such swift locomotion. The wind kissed my cheeks and the air was the perfect temperature—all by design.

As I flew, bits and pieces of my recent encounter with the watchers trickled into my thoughts and I shuddered. I had failed, and now I had no idea what to do.

Rather than heading straight towards the temple, I hovered in the air and stared outward with a critical eye, wondering how far out the prison extended. I could see miles and miles of green stretching off into the distance, but I also noticed a faint ripple in the air that signified some kind of reflection. I'd inspected it before, only to find that it was some kind of illusion, and the moment I had touched it with my finger, I had found myself right back in the center of the prison.

I wondered if it was a dome like the one now covering Kansas City. No one could leave this place without my permission.

I frowned uneasily at a tangential thought. Could I bring all these demons to Kansas City to help with the war? Could they be trusted? Obie had been adamant that their time in prison had smoothed out their edges, but we were talking about some very serious, sadistic, twisted criminals. The worst of the worst. Solomon had obviously locked them away for very good reasons, and bringing an army of new dangerous, untrustworthy demons to a war zone seemed like a bad idea.

If they truly were reformed, they would do me no good.

If they were all lying about being reformed, I would be tossing a pack of starving hyenas into a herd of wounded gazelles.

"Decisions, decisions," I murmured to myself. Then I focused on my bond with Envy and made my way to her balcony in the penthouse of Solomon's temple. The lights in her neighbor's suite were on and I heard classical jazz drifting out from the balcony. I grimaced, wondering if the space belonged to Greed. Who else would move into the space next door to Envy? No one else was powerful enough to claim such a status. Were they?

I saw Envy and Obie hanging out on the deck sofas, chatting back and forth as they sipped on amber champagne. They smiled and waved as I landed. I frowned suspiciously at their happy demeanor. Then I glanced over at Greed's balcony. I could easily hop the railing and enter her suite.

Envy patted the couch, drawing my attention. "Join us, Callie."

I complied and sat down beside Envy with a sigh. They wore similar clothes to mine and I realized I was growing more familiar with the outfit because I didn't openly stare at their bared chests. Obie was a petite, blonde-haired beauty with perfect skin and solid black eyes. She smiled at me and handed me a flute of champagne. Then she lifted hers in cheers. Envy followed suit, so I lifted mine as well.

We took sips of our drinks and then I leaned forward to look Obie in the eyes. "Where is Greed, and why are you in such a good mood?"

She opened her mouth to reply but she was interrupted by a desperate wail from the penthouse next door. I instinctively started to rise from my seat but Envy placed a firm hand on my thigh and shook her head. Obie lifted a remote in her hand and pressed a button. The classical music grew louder, washing out the tortured cry. I arched an eyebrow at her as she set down the remote and smiled at me.

"Greed is watching *A Christmas Carol*. The fall of Ebenezer Scrooge, in her eyes."

I blinked. "What?"

Obie nodded. "It's on repeat. A story about a rich miser changing his greedy ways. She's in agony."

Envy leaned forward with a malicious grin. "Obie can distort time here, so Greed has been watching it all day and night for the equivalent of seven years now."

Obie batted her eyelashes at me. "Brainwashing is fun."

I burst out laughing. "Wow. That's...incredible. To be honest, I had no idea how we were going to punish her or Uriel," I admitted.

Obie's cheer soured at mention of Uriel. "He's a tricky one. I'm working him over the old-fashioned way. But you can bet your hoo-ha that I'll come up with something truly terrible for the stinker who killed my Solomon," she vowed, and I saw a crackle of power ripple across her eyes, looking like crimson lightning.

I nodded and smiled, hiding my shiver of trepidation at her tone, even though I agreed with her decision. Uriel had tortured Solomon to death, and I had absolutely no sympathy for him. But to see the bubbly blondie so vehemently vengeful was enough to make my hair stand on end. Even though I knew that deep down, Obie was one truly fucking horrifying demon. Everyone who had earned a spot here had been wicked, but they all seemed radically reformed after hundreds of years. "Great job on Greed." I turned to Envy. "Have you had a chance to talk to Greed about how to help Claire?" I asked.

Envy's smile crashed and burned and she shook her head sadly. "No," she whispered. "I...don't think there is a way to unbreak her, Callie," she said, wincing as if she fully expected me to strike her.

I stared at her for a few seconds, struggling to process her claim. I wanted to scream. To hit something. To do anything. But...there was nothing to do. Part of me knew Envy was right. The only way for Claire to get out of it was on her own. There wasn't always a magical solution. In fact, there was rarely a magical solution—just shortcuts, and those often managed to lure you deeper into the woods.

I let out a deep breath and nodded. "Okay. Could you keep trying for me?" I asked.

She squeezed my thigh reassuringly and pulled me in for a hug. "Of course, Callie."

After a few moments, I pulled away and wiped my nose and eyes. The painful memory of Claire had caught me entirely by surprise since I had been so focused on my other problems. The other two pretended not to notice my tears and averted their eyes. I blinked rapidly to clear my vision, and then I turned to Obie. She had gone through terrible grief recently as well. Losing Solomon had hit her hard. Apparently, the pair had been in a romantic relationship of some kind. I knew she had meant the world to him, and she had obviously reciprocated those feelings more than she had let herself believe. The punishment she would ultimately design for Uriel would be worse than anything I could imagine, I had no doubts. But I had another idea I needed to run by her.

I cleared my throat and met her eyes. "Hypothetically, what would happen if I took the prisoners out on a field trip?"

She dropped her flute of champagne and her mouth hung open as she stared at me in stunned disbelief. "I...we," she trailed off, apparently struck dumb. She closed her eyes and took a shaky breath. Her hand was trembling and she didn't seem to realize it. Envy held her breath beside me and watched Obie very intently. When she noticed my attention, she gave me a subtle nod of agreement that it was a good idea on my part.

Obie finally opened her eyes and licked her lips anxiously. "We would be honored to serve you, White Rose," she whispered as she gripped her knees so hard that her knuckles started to turn white.

25

I nodded pensively, making sure I appeared calm and almost disinterested, as if it was just an absent thought that had popped into my head. "What assurances would I have that everyone would obey?"

Obie leaned forward like our conversation had just transitioned into the most important job interview of her life. "The brands on our backs would not permit us to go against your wishes even if we wanted to," she said, and then she twisted in her seat to show me the tattoo on her lower back. It was a precise and almost perfect rune of her demonic symbol—her name. "It was branded with Solomon blood, so we are quite literally an extension of your will. You are our puppet master, in a way."

I frowned. "That's insane," I blurted. "Why would Solomon lock you all up if he could control you with his mind? He could have simply demanded that none of you do bad things anymore, right? Why build this place?"

Obie smiled at some unspoken nostalgia and shrugged. "Sol said that it was exhausting to keep track of everyone and that he constantly had to be engaged with us for our appetites not to wander. Idle hands are the Devil's workshop. We needed a purpose or else we started resorting to bad habits, which would ultimately lead to pain and agony as the rune punished us with extreme pain. That's actually why he built this place. It was more of a rehab clinic for him to let us rebels recover while also serving to give him time to perfect the tattoo and to make his life less chaotic." She saw the dubious look on my face and shrugged. "How hard is it to make sure you are *always* making the best decisions? Doing the right thing?" she asked rhetorically. I smiled at her, not needing to verbalize the obvious answer. "Now multiply that by *all* of us," she said, gesturing at the pool and lounge area far below. "He used to make us build things for him, but once we were finished building and teaching him our magic, he didn't really have any task to set us on, and he knew we would be walking targets if he let us stay in the mortal realm."

I leaned back in my seat and glanced at Envy. The Sin looked troubled to learn that Solomon had been so powerful. "My siblings would have killed him if they knew he had complete control over all of you," she finally said, shaking her head.

Obie grinned proudly. "The wisest king in the world was smart enough not to brag in public for precisely that reason. He kept his little army of rebels tucked away in paradise in case he or his descendants ever needed some muscle."

I almost flinched as she so casually described my loosely framed idea. "Did...he ever say it like that?" I asked. Obie cocked her head with a faint frown. "Did he ever call you his little army or that his descendants might one day need your help?" I asked as casually as I could manage.

Obie nodded eagerly. "Oh, gosh yes. Tons of times. He fantasized about it all the time. We even play war games here once a week."

My eyes widened and I felt my breath catch. "War games?" I whispered. "You...can still..." I trailed off, not knowing exactly how to phrase my question. "You can still shift into your demon form and use your abilities without letting them control you?"

She nodded excitedly and let out a bubbly laugh. "We are men and women of virtue, now. We are beautiful monsters!" She cheered, and then she took a big sip of her champagne.

This time, my heart started racing wildly and I felt my stomach lurch. Azazel had said something very similar about being a man of virtue yet remaining a monster. Was that a coincidence? I couldn't exactly bring it up without giving Envy a heart attack. She would demand that I take her to him, yet there was still the teenie-weenie detail that he and his brother had murdered and eaten Archangel Raphael.

It wouldn't be the first dead archangel on my conscience, but it would definitely—

I blinked as an icy shiver rolled down my spine. Sanguina had dropped something into my hand before urging me to run. It...had felt suspiciously like a ring. Had she given me Raphael's freaking Halo? Holy crap.

Or maybe it was my imagination. Maybe one of my rings had fallen off and she'd simply returned it. I had appeared here at Solomon's Prison without meaning to. Maybe she'd scooped up the Seal of Solomon. It could have fallen from my finger when Samzaya destroyed the fiery swords. I grimaced at that unpleasant reminder as well, but I shoved it deep down before despair took over.

I'd just have to check when I returned.

"Where did you come up with the virtue comment?" I asked her with a warm smile. "I swear I've heard something like it before," I asked in a leading tone, scrunching up my forehead in a semblance of deep thought.

Obie waved a hand. "I'm sure you heard it a lot, hanging around Solomon." She cleared her throat and mimicked an old man's authoritative voice, complete with a stern frown and a waggling finger. "No tree can reach Heaven if its roots don't also reach Hell. Tradition isn't the worship of ashes; tradition is the preservation of fire. Only conscientious monsters can be virtuous." She burst out laughing, but the sound soon shifted to sorrow as she was reminded that Solomon was no longer with us. She took a drink of her champagne to hide her emotions.

I reached out and squeezed her knee sympathetically. "I miss him too, Obie," I said. I'd never heard Solomon give any one-liners like that, reminding me of how little time I had spent with my ancestor. I really had been a crappy descendent. I made the mental effort to stop taking shots at myself. Enough other people were doing it for me, so there was no reason to be a glutton for punishment.

She didn't meet my eyes, but she nodded and sniffled faintly. "If he would have just kept some of us out in the world by his side, we could have kept him safe. Stubborn old fool," she said in a sad rasp.

I gave her a few moments of privacy as I motioned for Envy to follow me to the balcony. "We'll be right back, Obie," I assured her. "I wanted to ask her a personal question anyway."

Obie mumbled something vaguely affirmative, so I tugged Envy after me. I paused at the balcony and stared out at the prison grounds—much smaller than they appeared to be. Naked people frolicked, danced, laughed, and splashed far below. Monstrous demons abstaining from violence, yet they could flip a switch to activate devil-mode.

Envy read my thoughts. "Theoretically, it makes perfect sense, but the amount of power that would have required is astonishing. Then again, we're talking about Solomon. He probably used demons as batteries to figure it out. He wasn't so kind and forgiving in his early years. I don't blame him for it, but it's an undisputed fact," she added, noticing my defensive frown. "Anyway," she continued, "they could be a big help in the war, but who would you send them against? If you sent them against Heaven or the Conclave, it will only reaffirm their claims that you side with Hell and need to be put down. If you send them against Hell, you'll only cause them to panic and double-down on how dangerous you are to their cause." She laughed coldly. "And I think the Horsemen have already come up with enough reasons to want you dead."

"Gee. Thanks for the pep talk," I muttered, even though I was actually wondering how to bring up my first meeting with her lover and his brother.

She shrugged. "I'm not saying it's a bad idea, just that there will be big consequences. On the other hand, doing nothing will likely result in your side losing, so..." She shot me a sympathetic smile and shrugged again.

I took a deep breath and decided to just speak plainly without fanfare. "I need to tell you some things, Envy, but I won't tell you if you can't control your reaction. I need you level-headed right now. Deal?"

She frowned pensively and stared into my eyes. Finally, she nodded. "Okay, Callie."

"Raphael is dead, and everyone is going to think I am responsible," I told her, carefully watching her reaction.

She swallowed audibly and then licked her lips, processing the big picture of such an event. "That is going to kick the war out into the open. Up until now, it's all been on the edge with unofficial skirmishes and battle lines drawn in chalk. Every one is trying to make the least regrettable alliances in order to achieve their unspoken long term goals."

"In summary, it's a clusterfuck. So why are any of them even here? Why did the Sins and Archangels come to Kansas City in the first place? You've dodged the question every time I've asked, but I'm no longer asking nicely, Envy. I demand an answer right this minute. A lot of people are going to die because of your arrival," I took a step forward and gripped her by the chin to get right up in her face, "and a lot of people who are very important to me have *already* died, and now you're saying this hasn't really been a war or a battle. That each side has their own long-term plans yet they aren't making any official moves." I slowly shook my head and let her see the resolve in my eyes. "Solomon, Last Breath, David and Greta, possibly Claire, and many, many more. We had to kill children today, Envy. Children!" I shouted, panting furiously. "So. Why did you come?"

I shoved her head to the side, took a step back, and then folded my arms.

Envy hung her head, knowing that I might have claimed that I had forgiven her for many crimes, but that some of them would not ever be forgiven or forgotten no matter how hard I tried. She'd wanted to make amends and clean her slate, but that was easier said than done. I hated that she was right.

I sensed a presence behind me and I turned to see Obie staring at me. What I hadn't expected to see was her wearing a red leather bodysuit with her blonde hair pulled back in a long, tight braid.

I also hadn't anticipated her new pet, since she hadn't said a word about it to me. She held a short leash that extended to a man in assless chaps on all fours who was groveling at my feet. He wore a leather studded collar, except his neck had streamers of fresh blood dripping down his skin, letting me know the collar was spiked on the inside. His long hair had been shaved in patches, looking like he'd survived a drunken bar fight with Edward Scissorhands. The barber's blades had struck skin in places, leaving behind a handful of puffy red wounds on his scalp. Other chunks of his hair had been dyed in garish bright colors purposely chosen to look ridiculous. He was covered in blisters and his entire body was beet red from the world's worst sunburn. His lower back featured a tattoo like everyone else, but his was green and gold and looked more intricate than the demon names. It seemed that Obie had been bluffing when she told me she hadn't yet figured out what to do with Uriel. He lifted his head to look at me with sheer and utter hatred and I found myself smiling approvingly. Obie yanked on the leather leash and Uriel cried out as the spikes from the collar tore into his flesh.

"It doesn't look upon the White Rose without Obie's permission!" Obie barked.

Uriel hung his head in shame and anger, but his obedience was remarkably ingrained. "Yes, Mistress Obie," he croaked.

26

Envy stared down at Uriel in disbelief. Her mouth was moving wordlessly and I couldn't blame her. Apparently, Obie hadn't told her about Uriel's accommodations.

I turned to Obie and admired her red leather. "That was an insanely fast wardrobe change." She grinned and gave me an eager nod, causing her braid to swing from side-to-side. "Where'd you get this idea from? I'm curious, because you were just complaining about not knowing what to do with him," I said.

Obie smiled. "Mistress Cara from the Sword of Truth books. Solomon used to read them to me, and the Mord-Sith...inspired our romance." Her grin deepened. "Inspired a lot of things, actually," she admitted.

I burst out laughing as I pointed down at Uriel. "How's it feel, d-hole? You just can't avoid women making you look weak and pathetic." His lips curled back in a snarl as he shot me a glare, but he averted his eyes before Obie could humiliate him again. "Oh, don't worry, Uriel. People back on Earth are all talking about your heroic deeds. You're a legend. An inspiration and small-g god to soy-slurping, vegan-cultist, beta males everywhere."

The archangel's shoulders trembled with rage, but his fear of Obie was greater—which was what I had been trying to test. He had been shamed and semi-broken already, but he clung to the last of his hatred like a man clutching a life raft. I remembered Azazel's definition of virtue—a monster knowing when to show restraint. I didn't fully understand it, but I was beginning to see the rough edges of it. Uriel was a monster who pretended not to be. He also had no self-control. To him, the ends justified the means, like Thrasymachus in Plato's *Republic*—'might is right' had been his argument. That those with power were justified when they directly applied that power to take what they wanted by force.

That concept had been an easy one for me to deny, even as a child. The hint was in the word 'take.' Anyone who chose to take something without giving something of equal value in return was already on the wrong side of the law, literally and morally.

Also, power corrupts, but absolute power corrupts absolutely.

That *definitely* described Uriel.

That kind of ingrained mentality would be almost impossible to break. It was his entire foundation of existence. He'd built everything else about himself from that bedrock, so there were no figurative home renovations in his future. Where Raphael had gone along with their crimes out of fear, Uriel had gone along with zeal, all too happy to bully those he considered beneath him.

Uriel liked to punch down rather than up. That told me everything I needed to know about his character.

I opened my mouth to press Envy on my original question, but Obie daintily cleared her throat. "Tell them why the Sins arrived, Uriel," she commanded of her slave.

When he didn't answer quickly enough, she gave a sharp tug to the leash and he yelped before figuratively tripping over himself to answer. "The Dark Horse prophecy!" he blurted. "They want to change Revelations!" he whimpered.

I knelt down and grabbed a fistful of his hair. Then I yanked it back, forcing him to stare up at me from a painful angle. "What is the Dark Horse prophecy?" I demanded, recalling Claire saying those exact words.

His eyes were wild and frantic as he stammered and sputtered, "I don't know! It's their prophecy, not ours. Something about tripping up Revelations so the book's predictions get knocked off track! It's their response to the Catalysts!"

Raphael's explanation of everyone panicking about the Catalysts echoed in my thoughts, matching up with Uriel's claim. I stared at him and imagined slamming his face into the floor. I knew it wouldn't hurt him since it wasn't possible to harm anyone here—

I frowned and looked up at Obie. "Hey. How are you able to hurt him? I thought that was impossible here."

She smiled. "We're opposites yet we're the same. The most harm a person can inflict is upon themselves. That's why Solomon preferred killing angels to bringing them here. It would only result in a never-ending battle between Heaven and Hell."

Even Uriel's eyes bulged at that, and he spun to give her a horrified look, but she yanked the collar hard before he could make eye contact. He fell to his face with a sharp cry as his neck bled copiously. I grimaced and rose to my feet. Then I turned to Envy and arched my eyebrow. "Well? What is he talking about? Why didn't you tell me you recognized the phrase Dark Horse?" I demanded, recalling Claire's eerie fever-dream.

Envy looked extremely nervous. "He speaks the truth, but I have never seen the prophecy. Only Wrath has. It might not even be real. It's more of a bedtime story he started telling us, that if we could mess up the beginning of the Apocalypse, we would alter the end. That it might protect us from the Catalysts." She shrugged helplessly, and I could tell she was genuinely frustrated. "Wrath encouraged us to join him in Kansas City, stating that he was destined to marry you and change our future. Then you denied him that opportunity and he fled. We've been unable—and unwilling—to return ever since. As soon as the archangels arrived, we could all sense the same thing and refused to leave. The end was here."

I folded my arms with a frown, wondering what the hell to make of this development. Was any of it true? I knew Envy wouldn't lie to me, and Uriel had only spilled the beans in hopes that it might buy him some leniency from Obie, but...

There was no real substance to it. I'd heard Wrath's dark prophecy before, but as soon as I'd turned Michael and Lucifer into an Anghellian, Wrath had fled with Gabriel. What did Gabriel have to do with the Dark Horse prophecy? How had creating an Anghellian messed that up?

On the other hand, it seemed to align with Raphael's explanation of recent history.

I started pacing, needing to exercise my body to kickstart my brain. I spoke out loud as I moved, turning on my heel to retrace my steps every ten feet or so. "The Conclave are useful idiots, thinking they are helping Heaven because they have blind faith. They also disagree with many of my actions, so predicting their allegiance is fairly self-explanatory," I murmured.

I saw Envy and Obie nodding but I ignored them. "Wrath failed to force me to marry him and then fled when I...created the Anghellian," I said, even though I hadn't really *created* anything; I'd just helped put them back together. "He's been missing ever since, even though he's obviously still pulling strings. Greed has nothing helpful to add to this?"

Obie grimaced. "She's currently in the mushed-pea stage of brain activity. Lots of weeping and uncontrollable screaming. She's of no use to anyone for at least a week."

I clenched my jaw and pointed at Uriel. "He seems pretty talkative. Do your time manipulation trick to speed up her healing."

Obie straightened her shoulders smugly. "He's an archangel. I have a natural affinity for breaking their faith in the natural order. I don't have to think of clever ways to punish him. I relied on the tried-and-true tactics of reeds shoved under the fingernails, whippings, occasional flaying, and sleep deprivation. Standard issue Hell stuff," she said with a dismissive wave of her hand, not realizing how truly horrifying it sounded.

Envy nodded matter-of-factly, looking bored.

"And the time manipulation only works on torture, not healing. Terrible ironies, right?" she added.

I shuddered and resumed my pacing. "Okay. Claire was taken by Greed and tortured practically to death. I've been told there is no hope for her recovery," I said, forcing the emotion from my voice even though my eyes were watering with tears. "But she reclaimed a moment of semi-lucidity this morning and mentioned the words Dark Horse, so I'm betting Greed was on the same bandwagon, and that was *after* Wrath's marriage proposal epically failed. So, Wrath is out there somewhere, and he's still thinking this prophecy will work in his favor." I scowled down at Uriel. "The fact that Gabriel is working directly with Wrath leads me to presume that there is something in it for Gabriel as well. Maybe he doesn't want Revelations playing out by the book either. But *why?*"

Envy shrugged, having already known these things. "It seems obvious why Heaven and Hell haven't truly gone to war, though. Their bosses—Wrath and Gabriel are working together behind the scenes. Has anyone seen Gabriel since he disappeared?"

We turned to Uriel who shook his head adamantly. "I have not. I swear.

With him out of the picture, I intended to take his place with the nephilim at my back. That's why I tried to take the fiery sword in the Garden," he admitted, sounding mildly ashamed. To me, it just came across as disappointed that his scheme hadn't worked.

I sneered. "You were the one who betrayed the nephilim in the first place. The Great Flood was supposed to wipe them off the face of the Earth, but you enslaved them!" I snarled.

He shook his head. "At Gabriel's command. That is why I went after them and against you. It would either give me the power to lead or it would make me valuable to Gabriel—"

Obie kicked him in the kidneys hard enough to crack a rib. She did it so casually that I flinched. Uriel crashed to the ground, unable to even scream as he writhed like an injured snake.

I scratched my chin thoughtfully, realizing that Uriel might have made a solid point. Gabriel was behind the nephilim fiasco long ago. If I took the nephilim, maybe it could draw Gabriel and Wrath out of hiding. They were the most valuable pieces on the game board. Them and my inmates here at Solomon's Prison. It didn't actually change anything because that had been my original plan.

Except that had been based on a defensive strategy. I hadn't considered it as an offensive strategy. Maybe that was why the Horsemen were so damned focused on me. They thought I was their lead to the Dark Horse prophecy. Or maybe I *was* the Dark Horse. Or all the Catalysts were, and they wanted to control us like they had with the nephilim. Regardless, my best bet was to get the nephilim on Team Callie. Especially after what I had seen at the Pearly Gates. I chose not to mention that for the time being. No reason to send everyone into a panic. I thought about how to convince Azazel and Samzaya to join my cause, and I had a sudden flashback of the shadow monster I had seen inside the sandstorm. I flinched involuntarily.

"Callie?" Envy asked, suddenly concerned as she reached out a hand to squeeze my shoulder.

I hung my head and gave her a weak smile. Then I glanced back at Obie. "Why don't you take Uriel back to his kennel. I still need to talk to Envy about something. In the meantime, I want you to prepare for that field trip." Her eyes beamed brightly and she nodded excitedly. "The next time I see you, it will probably be a call to war, but some will need to stay behind to look after these two."

Obie grinned toothily and Uriel looked like he wanted to vomit at the unanticipated overdose of FOMO that he just ingested. "The only way for anyone to get out of here is with your express permission. I could leave them here all by themselves and nothing would happen. In fact, it would be an excellent addition to their daily torture agendas."

Uriel actually moaned in horror. I ignored him and shot Obie a dubious look. "If you, a demon, can harm him because you are opposites, couldn't he do the same to you?"

Uriel grew suddenly still. Eerily still. Like a king cobra had just zeroed in on his genitals as a direct threat.

"Oh, Uriel!" Obie cheered in an overly eager tone. "Let's show her your *trick*!"

He shook his head and hunkered lower to the ground. "No. Please..."

✣ 27 ✣

She yanked the leash hard and he cried out, but she pulled him to his feet rather than permitting him to impersonate a maggot on the floor. He stood on shaky legs and faced her. Although he was significantly larger than her, his shoulders were slumped down and his back was hunched, taking a foot off his height. He looked more wretched and broken than his demeanor had led me to believe. Maybe he truly was utterly destroyed, and not as strong as I'd initially assumed.

"Hit me," Obie crooned, jutting her chin out towards him. "As hard as you can. I'll know if you hold back."

His whole body started to shake and I made the mistake of looking down, which rewarded me with a close-up look of his assless chaps. I grimaced and took a step back. Envy chuckled.

Uriel lifted a trembling fist and I noticed that he was panting hoarsely. Then he pulled back and swung at Obie's face, looking like he fully intended to decapitate her.

His fist stopped one inch away from her face and every bone in his wrist and hand shattered with a truly horrifying explosion of cracking sounds. Blood sprayed Obie's face and Uriel dropped to his knees with a silent, breathless scream as he held up his mangled fist. It looked like someone had taken a sledgehammer to it. Repeatedly.

The blood drained from my face and I almost gagged as I looked too closely at the mangled raw meat of Uriel's fist. I watched a few tiny bones fall to the ground with meaty splats and I heaved involuntarily. I felt suddenly dizzy and took a few steps back, forcing myself to look away. Obie was smiling down at Uriel. "Who's a good boy?" She asked him in a singsong tone. Her red eyes rippled with power and her face was speckled with the archangel's blood. She licked her lips and let out a purring moan of content as his blood hit her tastebuds. She looked over at me and grinned. "He has another hand if you want to see it again."

Envy grunted, looking surprisingly shaken. "Now I know why Solomon locked you up. We should have promoted you long ago." She didn't sound proud of this admission, but she had a solid point.

Obie curtsied and then scooped up the leash. Uriel was sobbing uncontrollably, looking like he'd lost that last little sliver of defiance in the exchange. "Come on, Uriel. I've got an ice-bath with your name on it. If you can stay in for one hour, I'll heal your hand. If you try to get out before the hour is up, you're going to have to hit me again with your broken hand. It will probably shatter your entire forearm. That would be a fun new experience, wouldn't it?"

"Y-yes, Mistress Obie," he croaked obediently, even though his eyes danced towards the balcony railing with a longing look, as if hoping he could throw himself over the edge. But he couldn't. I was fairly certain it would not kill him because Obie had likely established parameters to prevent him from committing suicide.

Obie winked at me. "The prisoners are no danger, White Rose. I'll rally the troops for our next great adventure!" Then she was frolicking away, tugging Uriel after her. His mangled hand left a trail of blood droplets in his wake. Within moments, it was just me and Envy on the balcony again.

I turned to her and let out a long breath, shaking my head in an attempt to banish any memory of the last five minutes. Even Envy looked startled by the Obie show. She shot me a crooked smile and brushed her red hair back over her shoulder. "Looks like you have your army. One of them." I could tell she was both eager and hesitant to hear what I wanted to share with her. "You said that Raphael had died and that you would take the blame for it..." she said, reminding me where we had left off.

I decided to get right to it. I had a lot to figure out back home and at the desert. "Azazel and Samzaya killed and ate Raphael," I said in a rush. She clutched a hand to her chest—which looked a whole lot stranger when there was no shirt involved, essentially cupping her boob for comfort—and her legs buckled as she let out a soft whimper. I caught her before she fell and then I steadied her by the shoulders. I led her towards the couch. "Let's sit down for this," I said in a gentle tone.

She complied, never taking her eyes from me as relief and concern warred across her face. I told her everything about Raphael, and my meeting with Azazel and Samzaya. I even told her about Azazel's cryptic comments at the end and how Samzaya very easily could have killed me had he wanted to. Then I told her about the fiery swords being destroyed.

Finally, I told her about what I'd seen at the Pearly Gates, which I was convinced had something to do with Wrath and Gabriel and their Dark Horse prophecy. Who else was strong enough to assault Heaven itself? If it was anyone, it was them. I'd just watched Raphael get turned into a pile of chum by two Watchers, so I didn't have high expectations of the other Sins and Archangels. The only other group who might have been strong enough to attempt such a brazenly suicidal attack would have been the Four Horsemen themselves.

And that was too chilling of a thought to entertain. Was that why they were after me? Were they behind it all? I didn't voice that concern to Envy, choosing to stick to the facts.

She listened intently without saying a word, looking shaken to her core. When I was finished, she remained silent for a full minute, blinking slowly like she was waking up from a deep sleep.

"You okay?" I asked, feeling concerned. "I was kind of hoping for you to cheer me up," I said with a hollow smile.

She blinked a few more times and then let out a long breath. "What if he's no longer the man I remember?" she whispered. "What if he's broken like Greed and Uriel?"

I nodded, seeing no reason to deny the obvious. "It would be understandable. But he looked entirely sane, and his parting words were meaningful and spoken with deep intent." I shrugged. "If they were raving lunatics, they would have killed me. They didn't. I can only hope that means I have a chance." I reached out to grip her hands in mine. Then I squeezed them. "But I think I'll need your help. Maybe having you with me would help convince them."

In reality, I had no idea if that would help or make everything worse. It really was my only option, though.

Envy nodded stiffly. "Of course. I...can do that," she said in a distant whisper, not sounding too sure of the outcome herself. "I don't know what I can do to help if he's willing to murder an archangel without even pretending at an honorable fight. It seems like he just wants blood."

I nodded. "All we can do is try. It's called being brave."

She gave me a very dry look. "Sounds like stupidity to me."

I shrugged. "Being brave is what you call it if you can pull it off without dying." I leaned back into the couch, wondering how to best maneuver the minefield in front of me. "We're going to need a distraction. Something to keep everyone busy while we work on the watchers and try to get some answers on the Pearly Gates attack."

Her eyebrows furrowed and she leaned back in her seat. "That attack simply seems impossible. Even if Gabriel and Wrath had been working together, I don't see how they could have been strong enough to break down the gate, let alone make it into Heaven."

I nodded my agreement, even though she was the better authority on their abilities. It was mildly reassuring, but not enough to give me any relief. Because if they weren't strong enough by themselves, it meant they had made friends with an even more powerful group of bad guys who I didn't even know about yet. Sheesh. "Well, the timing seems to coincide with all the wandering angels crashing down to the city."

Envy nodded absently; she looked lost in her own mind. "Perhaps..."

Obie returned to the balcony, still wearing her red leathers. I smiled at her as I came to a decision that I would hopefully not regret. "No reason to wait, Obie. I want your demons to start hunting wandering angels. Immediately."

Her eyes lit up and she nodded enthusiastically. I told her all about the wandering angels and how to tell them apart from the normal ones, which was quite simple. Their robes were dirty and they were insane.

"How do I find you after?" I asked her.

She rushed forward and grabbed me by the hand. "It's easy-peasy. If you think it, we will come."

That sounded entirely too simple. "Don't take this personally, Obie, but I'm going to need some proof that this isn't some trickery on your part. I've been burned too many times to take anything on faith."

Obie laughed with joy. "Hello! Demon!" She chuckled, pointing at her own chest. "We take nothing on faith. Use me as a guinea pig and take me back with you. Think some type of command in your mind and see if I obey. You'll instantly know I'm lying if I don't hear your command or don't follow it to the letter."

I shot Envy a questioning look and she nodded. "She's branded with Solomon's cockseye." My eyes bulged in surprise at her out-of-the-blue cursing, and then they shifted to Obie, who looked both proud of Envy's bizarre statement yet saddened at the reminder of Solomon's death. Envy winced at Obie. "Sorry, Obie."

Obie waved a hand and shrugged sadly. "I'll just take it out on Uriel later."

Envy noticed that I was still confused and she smiled in amusement. "Her tramp-stamp. Solomon's bullseye for his favorite appendage's favorite target," she clarified in a dry tone, pointing at Obie's rear.

Obie turned and wiggled her butt playfully. "She's not wrong."

I let out a groan and shook my head. "Let's get back on point here, girls."

Obie nodded and grabbed my hand, motioning for Envy to do the same. "Take us back to your body and think of a command."

I took a deep breath, hoped for the best, and closed my eyes. I almost popped a blood vessel trying to will myself back to my body, since I had no idea what I was doing. I'd come here by accident after nearly freezing to death in the watchers' prison.

I felt a faint pop in the air followed by a crackling sound. It sounded strangely similar to those old static channels that televisions used to have.

❧ 28 ❧

I woke up with a gasp and sat up straight as I jerked my head left and right in a panic. I was in a tent and I saw Gunnar and Alucard jump to their feet with shouts of relief. I clenched something tightly in my fist so hard that my nails had started digging into my palm. I opened them to see a golden Halo that I didn't recognize. Raphael's Halo! I looked back up at Gunnar and Alucard to tell them the good news, but I froze at the looks on their faces.

They were staring at something behind me, and then all hell broke loose. Alucard's hands burst into flames and Gunnar exploded into his werewolf form, and then they lunged towards me with bestial roars. I flung up a shield in front of them on instinct, knocking them back on their asses. Alucard's lava shot up high and lit the tent on fire, while Gunnar flew into the canvas wall and got tangled up. He snarled and growled as he tried to slash his way out of the burning, smoking tent. I risked a quick glance over my shoulder and almost soiled my pants to see a giant horned Elder—a lizard-human hybrid like Nate's friend, Carl—standing directly behind me. I tried to scramble away from the assassin and ended up rolling off the table I'd been sleeping on.

The tent was now completely on fire, which wasn't helped by Alucard flinging more lava balls in seemingly every direction, and Gunnar sounded like he was even more entangled than before. The horned Elder smiled wickedly and scooped me up off the ground. I hurled a blast of napalm fire at him and it sailed directly through his chest without even a whisper of resistance.

No. *Her* chest.

I was so startled that my magic had failed me that it took me a moment to realize she had flung me over her shoulder and was goddamned running away with me.

Help me, Obie! I thought as loudly as I possibly could. *A giant lizard bitch is kidnapping me and she's immune to magic!*

The Elder laughed triumphantly as she sprinted out of the raging inferno and into the cool desert night. I summoned my claws and started slashing wildly at my captor, stabbing the blades deep into my assailant's shoulders. But, like my magic, my blades sunk deep into her scales without any resistance, almost like I was trying to murder smoke.

What is this fucking thing, Envy? I demanded. *How do I kill it?*

Envy chuckled wickedly. *How about you just ask Obie not to save your life*, she said in a mocking tone.

I blinked stupidly as I continued flopping up and down on the Elder's back. Wait. The Elder was *Obie*?

Put me down, Obie. Now.

The Elder skidded to a halt and gently set me down. Then she gripped me by the shoulders to steady me and she even fixed my hair and rubbed a smudge of some unseen substance off my cheek like she was a fussy grandmother. I stared at her in disbelief, clearly verifying that she was an Elder and not like any demon I had ever seen. Her resemblance to Carl was uncanny. She was taller and skinnier, and had more spikes around her eyes— as well as her massive horns that reminded me of a dragon—but she was undeniably an Elder.

"Obie?" I asked, staring into her reptilian eyes.

The Elder curtsied and then let out a familiar bubbly laugh. "At your service, White Rose. Did I get your commands right?"

I nodded woodenly, realizing she had done everything I'd asked. I heard Gunnar howl from behind me and then I heard Alucard let out a hunting cry. "It's a lady Carl! Kill it!"

I spun and held out my hands before waving them frantically as I saw Gunnar and Alucard sprinting towards me. "Lady Carl is a friend named Obie!" I shouted at them as I shoved Raphael's Halo into my pocket. I wasn't sure why my direct contact with the ring hadn't activated the spirit of Raphael past. "She was trying to save me from the fire!" I explained.

They skidded to a halt and stared at me in surprise. Then they shifted their attention to Obie and stared even harder. Alucard shook his head after a few moments, lowering his lava hands. "Since when did you befriend a fucking Elder?" he demanded.

The tent behind them collapsed, sending up a spray of sparks as it continued to burn with a steady crackling sound. I glanced over my shoulder at Obie and motioned her forward. She stepped up beside me and waved one of her lethal claws at Gunnar and Alucard. "My name is Obyzouth and I used to have regular sex with King Solomon. Now I do what she says," Obie said, pointing a thumb at me.

Alucard sputtered incredulously and Gunnar promptly sat down on his haunches, looking confused. "Well, I guess that's better than having *irregular* sex with the old man," Alucard finally said.

Obie grinned and leaned a little bit closer to me before speaking out the side of her mouth. "Can I pet the hairy one with the missing eye? I always loved the rescue pets. A girl needs a project, right?" she whispered, except she did it loud enough for everyone to hear.

Alucard burst out laughing and nodded his agreement. "Yes. *Please* pet him. He only growls because he cares. I promise."

I shook my head at Obie, just in case she took him literally. The only other Elder I had met was Carl, and he was literal to an absolute fault. It was so easy to convince him of something that it was almost concerning. And since Obie was apparently an Elder, I wasn't sure how many of her characteristics from Solomon's Prison might have gotten lost in transmutation here to the real world.

Gunnar scowled at her. "I'm a werewolf. Not a rescue dog."

Obie clapped a claw over her mouth in embarrassment. "Oh, gosh! Sorry! Do you have any books here?" she asked eagerly as she took a quick step forward.

Gunnar's ear folded back on instinct and he growled warningly as he hunched lower, looking ready to defend his territory. "Back off, lady Carl," he growled. "I don't like to share."

Obie narrowed her eyes dangerously. "Be careful, werewolf. Disrespect pays dividends."

Alucard grunted. "Oh, I *like* that. Lady Carl is much smarter than our Carl."

Obie shifted her ire towards the vampire and her eyes narrowed even further.

"Hey, morons," I snapped. "How about you stop offending my friend by calling her lady Carl. Her name is Obie. Get it wrong again and I might decide to help her whoop your asses."

The pair of them mumbled an apology, and then Gunnar turned and loped towards the burning tent. He got down on all fours and...

"No way," I said.

Alucard turned around, took one look at Gunnar, and then he burst out laughing. "Where's a phone when you need one?" he hooted. "Nate has to see this." Because Gunnar was using his front paws to flick sand back behind him like a dog digging up a bone or trying to cover up his fresh poop. Gunnar's ears wilted under Alucard's laughter, but he kept right on going, flinging buckets of sand back on the fire to put it out.

✌ 29 ☙

In less than a minute, he'd doused the fire completely, leaving behind only charred fabric and a whole lot of smoke. I motioned for Obie to follow me as I jogged towards the burning remnants. Obie had covered a good amount of distance in her brief fire-rescue career. Alucard jogged over to my other side and shot me a meaningful look, as if to verify that I truly was safe and not a captive of Obie.

I smiled reassuringly and nudged him with my shoulder as we finally reached the ruined tent. Gunnar shifted back to his human form, revealing a whole lot of bulging Viking muscles and other fresh man meat—which Obie seemed highly appreciative of. Even though Gunnar was a veritable powerhouse of muscles, compared to Obie's much taller and broader Elder form, he looked like a chew toy compared to her. Gunnar noticed her attention and actually covered up his chest and groin with an offended glare at the huge, horned-lizard-woman. Then he nervously backed away into another tent before tugging the flap closed. I elbowed Obie and shook my head at her.

"Sorry," she apologized. "Been a *while*, you know?"

Alucard snorted in stunned disbelief. "Did she really have sex with Solomon?" he asked incredulously. "I thought she was just mixing up her words like Carl always does."

I shook my head. "Nope. Obie is one of the most literal people I've ever met, but she doesn't mince words. To be fair, she's a very dangerous demon who was locked away inside the Seal of Solomon," I said, showing him the large silver ring on my finger. "Inside the prison, she's a smoking hot blonde human. I had no idea what her demon form was until moments ago."

Alucard scratched his head in bewilderment, frowning at my ring. "You have a bunch of cute demons inside your ring, and you never told me about this?" he asked, sounding hurt.

Obie leaned towards him and flicked her tongue out suggestively. "We're all topless and frisky, too."

Alucard flung his hands up in outrage. "What the *fuck*, Callie? How could you do me like that? Do you have any idea how long I've been single?" he roared, way angrier than I would have thought.

I stared him directly in the eyes for a few seconds and then I slowly pointed my thumb at Obie. "Did you *want* me to introduce you to dozens of beautiful topless girls like her, Alucard?" I asked in a warning tone. "Because they're all still there, just waiting for a little fun from naive little human boys like you."

Obie laughed. "They would gobble you down and suck your bones clean, vampire. Be careful what you wish for."

Alucard's anger had faded under my glare, but Obie's comment brought his roguish grin back. "Well, don't threaten me with a good time, Obie. We only just met."

Gunnar exited the tent, now wearing sweats and a tank top. "Okay. Let's play—"

"Fetch!" Alucard interrupted in a rush, and then he pumped his fist to an invisible audience.

Gunnar rolled his eye and let out a resigned sigh. "The twelfth time is even funnier than the eleventh," he said drily. Then he shifted his critical gaze back to Obie and then me. "Let's play twenty questions," he said. "Because every time I think I'm doing the right thing by leaving my wife and children alone in St. Louis to help you out here in Kansas City, events take a completely ridiculous turn and—"

A small bear suddenly did a cartwheel directly between us, cutting Gunnar off. The bear did two more back-to-back before Alucard pointedly cleared his throat. The bear came to a stumbling halt and looked up sharply. He wore a plastic sparkly tiara on his head and he had a pungent cigar clamped between his teeth.

Starlight studied each of us like we were inanimate objects he hadn't noticed until this very moment. He literally hadn't even seen or heard us talking. His eyes finally settled on Obie and he took a step back. "Whoa," he murmured, plucking the cigar out of his mouth. I caught a whiff of the smoke on the breeze and realized it wasn't a cigar at all. It was a fat blunt. The devil's lettuce. He flung it to the side, shook his head clear of the concerning vision he'd just observed, and then he resumed his cartwheel routine off into the distance to work off his bad high.

Gunnar pointed angrily. "See? That's *exactly* what I'm talking about. You almost died inside that arctic sandstorm, and then you wake up with a giant —" He stopped to take a deep breath and dipped his chin politely at Obie. "You wake up with the wonderful Obie at your side and one of our tents burns down. Now, as weird as *that* sounds, we're still trying to figure out where Raphael is, why the rift didn't close, and why the Divines are all unconscious. Well, other than Lucky. He's exhausted but he's awake, yet he has no idea what happened in there either. We tried entering again and it seems to be warded even though we can see the rift right in front of us." He folded his beefy arms. "So, Callie. Why am I not playing with my kids at home right now? If you recall, I have plenty of family time to make up for. My kids need their father now more than ever, and I can honestly say I have no idea why I'm here or what we're even trying to accomplish. Give me a target already!"

Alucard stepped forward and placed a comforting hand on Gunnar's shoulder. "Easy, brother. You're not wrong, but Callie isn't the enemy." I frowned to see that Alucard was actually holding out a candy bar to Gunnar in his other hand. "Eat this, big guy. You'll feel less like a diva—"

Gunnar grabbed the chocolate and then punched Alucard in the gut hard enough to drop him to his knees. Alucard choked hoarsely and Gunnar took a big bite of the candy bar with a satisfied smirk. "You know what, Alucard? You're right," he said while chewing. "I feel better now."

Alucard waved a hand in a gesture that seemed to say *you're welcome*, but he was unable to speak.

Gunnar glanced at Obie and then handed her the chocolate bar. "Try this, Obie. You'll love it."

She took the chocolate with an excited smile and then she tossed the wrapper and chocolate all into her mouth. I saw her swallow and I was fairly certain she hadn't chewed it at all. Her eyes bulged and she let out a purring moan. "Oh, gosh!" she squealed. Then she wrapped Gunnar up in a bearhug and kissed him on the mouth.

Gunnar's eye was as big as I'd ever seen as he suffered the demon's gratitude without complaint. I peeled Obie off him and smiled. "That's good, Obie. No need to collect a restraining order your first day back."

She ducked her head apologetically and then shot Gunnar a thumbs up.

Gunnar smiled crookedly and turned back to me. He let out a guilty sigh and hung his head. "Sorry, Callie. I really miss my family, but that isn't your problem. On the other hand, my questions do warrant serious answers."

I nodded. "Let's go have a chat inside one of the other tents and I'll tell you everything I know." I thought about the new possibilities on the horizon with Obie and her demons on my side. "I think you really should go home, Gunnar. I can call you when I figure out what we're doing. If I need your help. Deal?"

He smiled eagerly and then gestured towards one of the smaller tents— the one he'd changed in moments ago. Then he kicked sand in Alucard's face just as the vampire was trying to get back up.

Alucard sputtered furiously and Gunnar grinned. "Fetch *that*, sunshine."

Obie smiled at the two childish men. "I like these two." Once inside the tent, I told them my plan. The word *plan* was an exaggeration. It was a gambit.

Gunnar was grinning like a buffoon. "Do you have any kids, Obie?" He asked excitedly.

The two of us winced and I set a hand on Gunnar's shoulder. "She...isn't that great with kids. Let's just leave it at that."

Gunnar frowned but ultimately shrugged before continuing on into the tent. Obie shot me a grateful look. From what I'd heard, Obie used to eat kids, so it was better for everyone if we left that little factoid in the past where it belonged.

✵ 30 ✵

fter a long discussion with Gunnar and Alucard, I sat in the sand, staring out at the strange black pyramid, waiting for some kind of message from Sanguina that it was safe for me to try and talk to the watchers. She didn't reply, but when I came too close to the pyramid she had sent me such a migraine that it made me see stars. Followed by a reprimand for me to be patient.

So, I'd decided to give Obie her wish, and now I was utterly exhausted from mentally keeping tabs on the dozen new sensations in my mind. It really was maddening to coordinate the demons unless I set them on a specific task with no room for deviance. Once I'd understood that, managing them had been fairly simple. I'd commanded them all to follow Obie's orders without question. Period.

Then all I'd had to do was give her very clear instructions on what to do, and what she was not permitted to do. So, now I was only juggling her thoughts in my mind.

And Envy.

And Sanguina.

And my own.

Obie's mission was to patrol Kansas City with her unit of fellow inmates, and hunt down and execute any and all wandering angels on a block-by-block basis. They were to kill them on sight and then loudly proclaim that they did so in service to the White Rose. If they encountered any other forces, they were to turn away and not engage—but only after openly acknowledging the opposing force. To look them in the eyes for a few moments, and then calmly walk away. I wanted my enemies to see my demons cleaning up the streets and intentionally not engaging with the Conclave, Heaven, or Hell. It would confuse the heck out of them.

It was also a way for me to test the limits of my new special forces, rather than letting all of them out and realizing my mistake too late. All I had to do now was manage Obie.

Still, I was utterly exhausted. Alucard sat beside me, brooding.

"I can't believe you unleashed a small army of pet demons on the city," Alucard said for the third time.

I turned to Alucard and sighed. "Only a dozen of them, and under very strict orders."

He shrugged. "You know it's still going to piss everyone off. It's going to make them look incompetent, which they will likely take great offense to."

I smiled. "I hadn't thought about that," I lied. "Darn."

He grunted, knowing me too well.

"I miss Gunnar," Alucard said.

I rolled my eyes, not looking over at him. "He's been back in St. Louis for less than an hour. I think you'll survive," I said drily. "He misses his family, and he's got kids to worry about now."

Alucard nodded. "Yeah, but now I have no one to play with," he muttered.

I laughed and shook my head. "The Divines are already awake and recovering. Enjoy the quiet. It's probably not going to last very long, and you'll wish you'd taken the time to appreciate it."

He let out a long suffering breath. "You going to try going in again?" he asked, obviously talking about the pyramid, and me convincing Azazel and Samzaya to help me.

I pursed my lips and stared at the pyramid. "When Sanguina gives me the all-clear," I told him. "She thinks they're too unstable at the moment."

Alucard nodded. "It doesn't sound like that is changing anytime soon, from what you told me."

This day felt like it had lasted for weeks. I frowned, feeling like I had forgotten something important, but I couldn't quite place what it was. I heard Starlight humming inside his tent behind us, but it didn't ring a bell. I reached into my satchel to grab my phone out of habit, and then my eyes widened.

I had completely missed my date with Ryuu.

I jumped to my feet and pulled out my phone. Of course, there was no service in the Sahara desert. I hadn't just missed our date. I had missed it by hours and hours. Had he called?

"Shit. I need to go back to Kansas City. Ryuu is probably worried sick. I was supposed to meet him earlier."

Alucard nodded and waved a hand. "I'll be here when you get back. I'll probably be doing exactly this," he grumbled, scooping up a handful of sand and flinging it in front of him.

"Right. I'll be back soon. Don't let anyone inside, okay?" I asked, pointing at the pyramid.

He shot me a dubious look. "Why? They would freeze to death after ten feet."

He had a solid point, but it felt dangerous to leave it open like this, even though no one even knew we were here in the first place. "I'll send someone up here to join you," I said, chewing through a list of names to see who I trusted with this kind of secret. Everyone with that level of trust was needed on the battlefield. Gunnar and Alucard had been perfect guardians because their Horsemen Masks limited their usefulness in the fight against Heaven and Hell.

I Shadow Walked to Xuanwu's estate since that was where we had initially agreed to meet. As expected, he wasn't sitting on the porch waiting for me. I checked my phone and frowned, not seeing any missed calls. I rushed up to the door and lifted my hand to knock when a voice called out from behind me.

"Finally," a man said. "I was beginning to think you didn't care about him."

I stiffened, realizing the voice was referring to Ryuu. I slowly turned around. Death stood on the sidewalk, and he held his giant scythe at his side. I narrowed my eyes and took a few steps closer. "What can I do for you, brother?" I asked, my voice dripping with disdain. He was all alone. I somehow managed to keep my composure, knowing that I had entirely too many secrets on my mind to lose control. If I slipped up, Death would learn some things I couldn't risk him knowing.

He stared back at me in silence. "Where is Raphael?"

I glared back at him. "We parted ways after our private chat. Why?"

"Because he was supposed to bring you to the hearing."

I shook my head. "I don't do hearings, Death."

He nodded slowly. "I'm beginning to realize that, Callie Penrose. But now people are beginning to ask about Raphael. It seems no one has seen him since your little stunt. And that little gift you left behind at the orphanage is also...ruffling many feathers. On both sides of the figurative aisle."

I nodded. "That was kind of the point. I didn't do it because I was bored." I scanned the area behind him. "Let's cut to the chase. Where is Ryuu?" I asked in a low, warning tone.

Death smiled, his skeleton mask somehow shifting to accommodate such a motion. "He's waiting for us. Let's go somewhere a little less...breakable." I took an aggressive step closer and he held up a skeletal finger. "His life depends on your compliance, White Rose. We tried this the easy way. Welcome to the hard way."

I gritted my teeth and struggled to control my breathing. "I'm listening," I growled.

"Meet me at the orphanage," he said. Then he turned his back on me and started walking away. "Five minutes." Between one step and the next, he disappeared.

I let out a feral scream and glared at the spot where the Horseman of Death had been standing. Then I dialed Ryuu on my phone, wondering if this was some kind of deception. How in the world had Ryuu, of all people, been abducted. His phone went straight to voicemail.

"I'm going to kill him," I snarled.

Easy, Callie, Envy urged, sounding troubled. *Take a breath*.

"I'm trying!" I snapped, panting wildly. I probably only had four minutes now. "He can't possibly want to arrest me this badly," I growled, shaking my head. "He knows me well enough to understand that I would kill him over this, so why would he push this hard? What is so damned important about this stupid mistake I made with my mask?" I demanded.

I...do not know, Envy admitted.

I sat down in the grass and forced myself to meditate. I only had minutes to get to the orphanage, but sometimes thirty seconds of extreme focus could make all the difference in the world—ask most men. I didn't even bother with the complicated stuff. I just sat there and cleared my mind completely, focusing only on breathing in and out. I felt my pulse slowly steadying and my shoulders relaxing. I kept going, imagining me facing Death in front of the orphanage. I imagined me defeating him, and accepting the fact that one of us might die, depending on what he had in store.

I committed myself to killing the Horseman of Death.

I opened my eyes and calmly rose to my feet, listening to the birds chirping in the nearby trees, and appreciating the gentle breeze on my cheeks.

I smiled to myself.

"It is a good day to die," I murmured out loud.

Then I Shadow Walked to the orphanage.

31

I arrived in the center of the street outside the blackened orphanage, and I was surprised to find the road completely cleared of bodily remains. As I'd expected, the building had not fallen since it was almost entirely made of stone. It looked like a stone skull with all of its windows and doors burned away.

What I had not expected was the crowd of observers.

I sent a thought out to the ether, just to keep things interesting.

The Conclave forces filled an entire side street, all watching me in silence. On the opposite side of the street, I saw demons by the dozens standing behind three Sins in their black archangel armor. Gluttony, Lust, and Sloth. Wrath was not present.

Adjacent to them stood a mass of angels next to three white-armored Archangels. I recognized Ramiel, but I hadn't met the other two before. Between the forces of Heaven and Hell stood three of the Horsemen—War, Pestilence, and Famine.

They all stood well back from the street, leaving me plenty of room to put on a show, because Death stood twenty paces in front of me, waiting patiently with Ryuu at his side. Ryuu looked absolutely livid, and he had a bomb strapped to his chest. I met his eyes for only the briefest of moments, committing every detail to memory. Then I settled my stance and squared my shoulders as I turned to stare directly at the Horseman of Death.

This was to be a show trial. He had purposely invited everyone here to witness this. I didn't understand what he hoped to get out of such a plan, but I only had one outcome on my mind. I was a bullet aimed at a target. All that was left to do was pull the trigger.

Now, how I achieved that goal would determine many other events down the road. With this many witnesses, I was betting it wasn't a simple fight Death wanted. We could have done that at Xuanwu's estate. Death had wanted an audience, and he had made certain to absolutely guarantee that I showed up.

Why was that so important to him? I cleared my mind of all those questions and focused on the matter at hand. None of those questions mattered if I got myself killed today by being distracted.

Death met my eyes with a determined glare. "If he moves from that spot, the bomb goes off. If anyone tries to disarm or remove the bomb, it goes off. Do you have any questions?"

I gave him the barest shake of my head. I looked past him at the other three Horsemen. My voice rang out in a confident chime. "My condolences in advance."

The crowd murmured loudly at that, and the three Horsemen looked grim before quickly growing silent.

Death took a few steps away from Ryuu as he stared into my eyes. "Callie Penrose!" He bellowed in a voice loud enough for everyone to hear clearly. "You have been summoned here today—"

I drew my katana with a flourish and leveled it at him with a wicked smile. "I voluntarily *chose* to be your executioner," I clarified, speaking just as loudly as him, although I kept my tone calm and measured, signifying that I was clearly unimpressed by the festivities at hand. "Thank you for the honor."

His glare was smoldering, and I heard Gluttony laugh.

"What happened to Archangel Raphael?"

"We shared a meal with friends and then we parted ways," I replied calmly, not letting a flicker of unintended emotion break through my demeanor.

"No one has seen him since you abducted him," Death pressed.

I shrugged. "He must have found something more entertaining than watching an old dog be put down. Perhaps he likes dogs." I took another step towards him, still holding my katana at him. "Can we proceed?"

"You have been warned about abusing your responsibilities as one of the Dread Four and interfering—"

"Yep. Got it. I wasn't supposed to cross streams. Whoops." I advanced another step, grinning for the crowd. "Now. Here are my terms. You release Ryuu at this very moment or your brothers will have to pay the consequences for your egregious error in judgment. After I kill you, of course." The three Horsemen narrowed their eyes and took a step forward but Death waved them back. "Release Ryuu now and this ends with you, Death."

The angels and demons roared in both outrage and cheer, indicating there were different factions within each camp. They were not all of the same mind just because they were from the same neighborhood. Interesting. Surprisingly, the Conclave was the most reserved about the tense situation. I'd expected the Templars to start chugging beers and throwing beads or something. Or for the nephilim to flock to one particular archangel and give up the perpetrator behind the black cuffs.

Unfortunately, none of that happened.

Death pointed his scythe at me. "You stand alone, Horsewoman. What makes you think you have any authority to threaten my brothers—"

I held up a hand to silence him, and then I smiled toothily. I glanced over my shoulder at a sudden sensation. The street behind me was empty and dark.

For precisely five seconds.

Then a wandering angel flew out of the darkness and landed beside me with a sickening splat. He was missing his head. From the darkness, Obie and a dozen demons silently strolled forward. The only sound was the clacking of their claws on the pavement.

Oh, and they were fucking huge. One looked like a scaled bear, and he had to be at least twenty-feet-tall, even though he was currently walking on all fours. On his shoulders were two cat-like demons with antlers and slitted eyes. They were each the size of a car and heavily layered in muscle and armored skin.

Three griffins swooped up onto the ledges of the buildings above me and let out piercing screams.

Three more vibrantly turquoise-scaled Elders walked side by side, flicking their tongues hungrily.

Obie grinned excitedly and waved at the gathered crowds. "Long time no see! We were getting rid of the last of the wandering angels for the White Rose. Did we miss anything?"

I shook my head at her and winked before turning back around. "Nope. We were just getting to the good part," I told her as I stared into Death's eyes. "This is just between me and him, Obyzouth. Take a load off and enjoy yourselves."

Death gripped his scythe tightly and I knew I had won the crowd, even if the majority of them did despise or hate me. I'd made Death look like a fool, even after all of his careful planning. I still didn't know why he'd bothered with all of this, but we were well beyond that point now.

"What's it going to be, skull boy? Just you, or am I chopping down the rest of the family tree, too?"

He glanced back at his brothers, and in that moment he lost all credibility with the crowd he had gathered. He walked over to Ryuu and deactivated the bomb. Ryuu stared into his eyes with barely restrained fury, but I waved a hand at him and shook my head. This was no longer Ryuu's fight.

Death removed the vest and stepped back, gesturing for Ryuu to leave. The ninja glared at him for a few more seconds and then spat to the side in a disgusted gesture at Death's lack of honor for using Ryuu to get to me. Then Ryuu calmly walked up to my demons and clasped his hands behind his back as he faced us from the sidelines, looking like a martial arts instructor at a tournament, waiting to watch his student compete.

I dipped my chin at him and then turned to face Death for what seemed like the hundredth time.

Death lifted his scythe in a ready stance and met my eyes. I could have let him depart in shame, but that would have lost me the fear of the crowd. He also didn't deserve such an easy out because he had publicly used one of my people as a hostage. Anything other than extreme punishment would only encourage future enemies to try the same tactic.

I needed to shut that tactic down for good, and make everyone think twice about using my people as hostages. The Horseman of Death had to die.

I started walking towards him with a grim smile, and he did the same.

He swung out with his scythe and I blocked it with my katana in a bright flash of sparks. We stood there, straining against each other and staring into each other's eyes from inches away.

So it startled the living hell out of me when he murmured in a genuinely friendly tone full of sorrow. "Make it quick and absolute, Callie. They can have no doubts that you defeated me. This was the only way to make it work," he murmured, "since you refused to meet with me." I tried pulling away, not wanting to get sucked into his head games, but he grabbed my blade with his claw and pulled me close to prevent me from retreating. "Listen!" he hissed. "You need to *become* Death. My time is finished. I've known this day would come for many years. You must merge your mask with mine."

I kicked him in the chest and released my katana, forcing him to stumble back with my sword still in his hand. His eyes widened in confusion and then panic, although he regained his composure swiftly so the crowd did not notice. He flung my sword to the side. What the fuck was going on? I saw Ryuu in my peripheral vision, and he had a very troubled look on his face, sensing that something was not what it seemed.

I summoned my claws and rushed Death. He waited for me to get close before he started blocking each of my strikes with his scythe. "I won't play your games," I growled, careful to keep my words between us.

"The Pearly Gates are just the beginning," he said, staring directly into my eyes. "Kill me!" he begged. "Now! There is no more *time*."

"You betrayed us?" I hissed, stunned.

He shook his head discreetly. "No, child. This is a sacrifice for the greater good. The Four Horsemen must die at the hands of the Dread Four if you are to have a chance at winning the Omega War. Tell Nate that I'm proud of him, and that I'm sorry," he rasped, and I saw an actual tear fall from his skeleton mask, proving to me that this was no act of subterfuge. "You are now *Death*, Callie Penrose. Memento mori."

This was, in fact, Death's final act.

And then he gave me an opening.

I watched the tear fall, and I reacted on instinct. I lashed out with my claws, feeling numb and dead inside. My claws abruptly flared with the fires of Eden, startling the living shit out of me, as they tore through the Horseman of Death's throat.

There was no blood.

His arms went limp and he dropped his scythe.

His body fell back and I watched him crash to the ground in slow motion. My claws blazed with the fires of Eden, and I didn't even care. Death had...sacrificed himself, but for what? What chance? Why was time almost up? What the hell had he been so scared of?

And how was I going to tell Nate what I'd done?

That I'd killed one of his best friends.

That I'd killed one of the Four Horsemen.

Death stared up at the sky, his throat torn and charred from my fatal strike. I bent down and carefully pulled the Mask of Death off his face, feeling like the worst person in the world, even though I had to keep playing my part for the crowd. When the mask came free, I saw an old man smiling proudly up at the sky. His eyes were lifeless, but not a flicker of pain resided in them.

I reached down and slid my fingers over his face, closing them in respect. "I will miss you," I breathed.

Then I scooped up his scythe and rose to my feet. I stared down at the skeleton mask in my hand and nodded. Then I slipped it into my satchel, pretending I didn't want to vomit.

I hadn't even noticed Obie and her demons surrounding me in a protective ring. The remaining three Horsemen glared at me with pure hatred, but almost everyone else had fled on foot or taken to the skies.

I stared back at the Horsemen, careful to keep my face resolute and cold. The way they were glaring at me, and the way Death had put on such a show, I realized the unspoken part of his last words. He had not told his brothers that they all had to die.

That the Dread Four would have to kill them.

He'd known they wouldn't agree to it, so he'd needed to give them a reason to hate me. A grand display to convince them of the significance of this moment. He hadn't just sacrificed his life. He'd used himself as the fuse to turn the rest of his brothers against us as well. He'd made us enemies for the greater good.

And if that wasn't crazy enough, I had the eerie feeling that he was correct.

Because I felt the Omegabet carved into the haft of his scythe, and I realized it was his last words. I risked a quick glance and saw my name carved into the wood in a tiny scrawl. A message specifically for me.

I turned away from the Horsemen, knowing they would never forgive me and that I would probably never forgive myself for what Death had made me do.

But I walked back to Ryuu as a victor. I didn't embrace him. I paused a few feet in front of him and met his eyes. He recognized the pain I was trying to hold back and I saw him clench his jaw protectively, but he did not give in to those passions. I was obviously putting on some kind of show, which he had recognized from the fight itself.

He trusted me enough to go with it rather than ruin it for me.

He bowed respectfully and scooped up my discarded katana. He slipped it into his belt and watched me, letting me decide what happened next.

"Gather to me," I commanded in an authoritative tone. Obie and her demons rushed to comply until everyone was huddled around me. "Grasp hands. We're getting the fuck out of Kansas City. Things are about to go to hell and we have no time to waste."

Obie grinned hungrily and gestured at her demons to obey. Soon, we were all holding hands or at least maintaining physical contact. "Keep them in line, Obie. We're going to Castle Dracula." I glanced back at the Horsemen, who were still glaring at me with pure hatred. "The war just officially started."

I Shadow Walked us out of the City of Fountains, knowing things had changed forever.

I was the Horsewoman of Despair.

I was the Horsewoman of Death.

I had flicked the first domino, and I had no idea what was going to happen next.

The Horsewoman of Death will return in 2021...

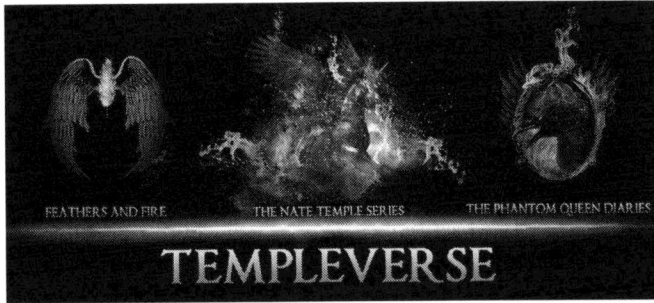

TEMPLEVERSE

Turn the page to read a sample of **OBSIDIAN SON** *- The Nate Temple Series Book 1 - or* **BUY ONLINE**. *Nate Temple is a billionaire wizard from St. Louis. He rides a bloodthirsty unicorn and drinks with the Four Horsemen. He even cow-tipped the Minotaur. Once...*

(Note: Nate's books 1-6 happen prior to UNCHAINED, but they crossover from then on, the two series taking place in the same universe but also able to standalone if you prefer)

Full chronology of all books in the TempleVerse shown on the 'BOOKS BY SHAYNE SILVERS' page.

TRY: OBSIDIAN SON (NATE TEMPLE #1)

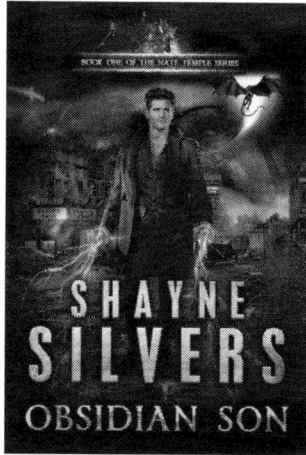

There was no room for emotion in a hate crime. I had to be cold. Heartless. This was just another victim. Nothing more. No face, no name.

Frosted blades of grass crunched under my feet, sounding to my ears like the symbolic glass that one would shatter under a napkin at a Jewish wedding. The noise would have threatened to give away my stealthy advance as I stalked through the moonlit field, but I was no novice and had planned accordingly. Being a wizard, I was able to muffle all sensory evidence with a fine cloud of magic—no sounds, and no smells. Nifty. But if I made the spell much stronger, the anomaly would be too obvious to my prey.

I knew the consequences for my dark deed tonight. If caught, jail time or possibly even a gruesome, painful death. But if I succeeded, the look of fear and surprise in my victim's eyes before his world collapsed around him, it was well worth the risk. I simply couldn't help myself; I had to take him down.

I knew the cops had been keeping tabs on my car, but I was confident that they hadn't followed me. I hadn't seen a tail on my way here but seeing as how they frowned on this kind of thing, I had taken a circuitous route just in case. I was safe. I hoped.

Then my phone chirped at me as I received a text.

I practically jumped out of my skin, hissing instinctively. "Motherf—" I cut off abruptly, remembering the whole stealth aspect of my mission. I was off to a stellar start. I had forgotten to silence the damned phone. *Stupid, stupid, stupid!*

My heart felt like it was on the verge of exploding inside my chest with such thunderous violence that I briefly envisioned a mystifying Rorschach blood-blot that would have made coroners and psychologists drool.

My body remained tense as I swept my gaze over the field, fearing that I had been made. Precious seconds ticked by without any change in my surroundings, and my breathing finally began to slow as my pulse returned to normal. Hopefully, my magic had muted the phone and my resulting outburst. I glanced down at the phone to scan the text and then typed back a quick and angry response before I switched the cursed device to vibrate.

Now, where were we?

I continued on, the lining of my coat constricting my breathing. Or maybe it was because I was leaning forward in anticipation. *Breathe*, I chided myself. *He doesn't know you're here.* All this risk for a book. It had better be worth it.

I'm taller than most, and not abnormally handsome, but I knew how to play the genetic cards I had been dealt. I had shaggy, dirty blonde hair—leaning more towards brown with each passing year—and my frame was thick with well-earned muscle, yet I was still lean. I had once been told that my eyes were like twin emeralds pitted against the golden-brown tufts of my hair—a face like a jewelry box. Of course, that was two bottles of wine into a date, so I could have been a little foggy on her quote. Still, I liked to imagine that was how everyone saw me.

But tonight, all that was masked by magic.

I grinned broadly as the outline of the hairy hulk finally came into view. He was blessedly alone—no nearby sentries to give me away. That was always a risk when performing this ancient rite-of-passage. I tried to keep the grin on my face from dissolving into a maniacal cackle.

My skin danced with energy, both natural and unnatural, as I manipulated the threads of magic floating all around me. My victim stood just ahead, oblivious to the world of hurt that I was about to unleash. Even with his millennia of experience, he didn't stand a chance. I had done this so many times that the routine of it was my only enemy. I lost count of how many times I had been told not to do it again; those who knew declared it *cruel, evil, and sadistic*. But what fun wasn't? Regardless, that wasn't enough to stop me from doing it again. And again. And again.

It was an addiction.

The pungent smell of manure filled the air, latching onto my nostril hairs. I took another step, trying to calm my racing pulse. A glint of gold reflected in the silver moonlight, but my victim remained motionless, hopefully unaware or all was lost. I wouldn't make it out alive if he knew I was here. Timing was everything.

I carefully took the last two steps, a lifetime between each, watching the legendary monster's ears, anxious and terrified that I would catch even so much as a twitch in my direction. Seeing nothing, a fierce grin split my unshaven cheeks. My spell had worked! I raised my palms an inch away from their target, firmly planted my feet, and squared my shoulders. I took one silent, calming breath, and then heaved forward with every ounce of physical strength I could muster. As well as a teensy-weensy boost of magic. Enough to goose him good.

"*MOOO!!!*" The sound tore through the cool October night like an unstoppable freight train. *Thud-splat!* The beast collapsed sideways onto the frosted grass; straight into a steaming patty of cow shit, cow dung, or, if you really wanted to church it up, a Meadow Muffin. But to me, shit is, and always will be, shit.

Cow tipping. It doesn't get any better than that in Missouri.

Especially when you're tipping the *Minotaur*. Capital M. I'd tipped plenty of ordinary cows before, but never the legendary variety.

Razor-blade hooves tore at the frozen earth as the beast struggled to stand, his grunts of rage vibrating the air. I raised my arms triumphantly. "Boo-yah! Temple 1, Minotaur o!" I crowed. Then I very bravely prepared to protect myself. Some people just couldn't take a joke. *Cruel, evil,* and *sadistic* cow tipping may be, but by hell, it was a *rush*. The legendary beast turned his gaze on me after gaining his feet, eyes ablaze as his body...*shifted* from his bull disguise into his notorious, well-known bipedal form. He unfolded to his full height on two tree trunk-thick legs, his hooves having magically transformed into heavily booted feet. The thick, gold ring dangling from his snotty snout quivered as the Minotaur panted, and his dense, corded muscles contracted over his now human-like chest. As I stared up into those brown eyes, I actually felt sorry...for, well, myself.

"I have killed greater men than you for lesser offense," he growled.

His voice sounded like an angry James Earl Jones—like Mufasa talking to Scar.

"You have shit on your shoulder, Asterion." I ignited a roiling ball of fire in my palm in order to see his eyes more clearly. By no means was it a defensive gesture on my part. It was just dark. Under the weight of his glare, I somehow managed to keep my face composed, even though my fraudulent, self-denial had curled up into the fetal position and started whimpering. I hoped using a form of his ancient name would give me brownie points. Or maybe just not-worthy-of-killing points.

The beast grunted, eyes tightening, and I sensed the barest hesitation. "Nate Temple...your name would look splendid on my already long list of slain idiots." Asterion took a threatening step forward, and I thrust out my palm in warning, my roiling flame blue now.

"You lost fair and square, Asterion. Yield or perish." The beast's shoulders sagged slightly. Then he finally nodded to himself in resignation, appraising me with the scrutiny of a worthy adversary. "Your time comes, Temple, but I will grant you this. You've got a pair of stones on you to rival Hercules."

I reflexively glanced in the direction of the myth's own crown jewels before jerking my gaze away. Some things you simply couldn't un-see. "Well, I won't be needing a wheelbarrow any time soon, but overcompensating today keeps future lower-back pain away."

The Minotaur blinked once, and then he bellowed out a deep, contagious, snorting laughter. Realizing I wasn't about to become a murder statistic, I couldn't help but join in. It felt good. It had been a while since I had allowed myself to experience genuine laughter.

In the harsh moonlight, his bulk was even more intimidating as he towered head and shoulders above me. This was the beast that had fed upon human sacrifices for countless years while imprisoned in Daedalus' Labyrinth in Greece. And all that protein had not gone to waste, forming a heavily woven musculature over the beast's body that made even Mr. Olympia look puny.

From the neck up, he was now entirely bull, but the rest of his body more closely resembled a thickly furred man. But, as shown moments ago, he could adapt his form to his environment, never appearing fully human, but able to make his entire form appear as a bull when necessary. For instance, how he had looked just before I tipped him. Maybe he had been scouting the field for heifers before I had so efficiently killed the mood.

His bull face was also covered in thick, coarse hair—he even sported a long, wavy beard of sorts, and his eyes were the deepest brown I had ever seen. Cow-shit brown. His snout jutted out, emphasizing the golden ring dangling from his glistening nostrils, and both glinted in the luminous glow of the moon. The metal was at least an inch thick and etched with runes of a language long forgotten. Wide, aged ivory horns sprouted from each temple, long enough to skewer a wizard with little effort. He was nude except for a massive beaded necklace and a pair of worn leather boots that were big enough to stomp a size twenty-five imprint in my face if he felt so inclined.

I hoped our blossoming friendship wouldn't end that way. I really did.

Because friends didn't let friends wear boots naked...

TRY: WHISKEY GINGER (PHANTOM QUEEN DIARIES BOOK 1)

The pasty guitarist hunched forward, thrust a rolled-up wad of paper deep into one nostril, and snorted a line of blood crystals—frozen hemoglobin that I'd smuggled over in a refrigerated canister—with the uncanny grace of a drug addict. He sat back, fangs gleaming, and pawed at his nose. "That's some bodacious shit. Hey, bros," he said, glancing at his fellow band members, "come hit this shit before it melts."

He fetched one of the backstage passes hanging nearby, pried the plastic badge from its lanyard, and used it to split up the crystals, murmuring something in an accent that reminded me of California. Not *the* California, but you know, Cali-foh-nia—the land of beaches, babes, and bros. I retrieved a toothpick from my pocket and punched it through its thin wrapper. "So," I asked no one in particular, "now that ye have the product, who's payin'?"

Another band member stepped out of the shadows to my left, and I don't mean that figuratively, either—the fucker literally stepped out of the shadows. I scowled at him, but hid my surprise, nonchalantly rolling the toothpick from one side of my mouth to the other.

The rest of the band gathered around the dressing room table, following the guitarist's lead by preparing their own snorting utensils—tattered magazine covers, mostly. Typically, you'd do this sort of thing with a dollar-bill, maybe even a Benjamin if you were flush. But fangers like this lot couldn't touch cash directly—in God We Trust and all that. Of course, I didn't really understand why sucking blood the old-fashioned way had suddenly gone out of style. More of a rush, maybe?

"It lasts longer," the vampire next to me explained, catching my mildly curious expression. "It's especially good for shows and stuff. Makes us look, like, less—"

"Creepy?" I offered, my Irish brogue lilting just enough to make it a question.

"Pale," he finished, frowning.

I shrugged. "Listen, I've got places to be," I said, holding out my hand.

"I'm sure you do," he replied, smiling. "Tell you what, why don't you, like, hang around for a bit? Once that wears off," he dipped his head toward the bloody powder smeared across the table's surface, "we may need a pick-me-up." He rested his hand on my arm and our gazes locked.

I blinked, realized what he was trying to pull, and rolled my eyes. His widened in surprise, then shock as I yanked out my toothpick and shoved it through his hand.

"Motherfuck—"

"I want what we agreed on," I declared. "Now. No tricks."

The rest of the band saw what happened and rose faster than I could blink. They circled me, their grins feral...they might have even seemed intimidating if it weren't for the fact that they each had a case of the sniffles —I had to work extra hard not to think about what it felt like to have someone else's blood dripping down my nasal cavity.

I held up a hand.

"Can I ask ye gentlemen a question before we get started?" I asked. "Do ye even *have* what I asked for?"

Two of the band members exchanged looks and shrugged. The guitarist, however, glanced back towards the dressing room, where a brown paper bag sat next to a case full of makeup. He caught me looking and bared his teeth, his fangs stretching until it looked like it would be uncomfortable for him to close his mouth without piercing his own lip.

"Follow-up question," I said, eyeing the vampire I'd stabbed as he gingerly withdrew the toothpick from his hand and flung it across the room with a snarl. "Do ye do each other's make-up? Since, ye know, ye can't use mirrors?"

I was genuinely curious.

The guitarist grunted. "Mike, we have to go on soon."

"Wait a minute. Mike?" I turned to the snarling vampire with a frown. "What happened to *The Vampire Prospero*?" I glanced at the numerous fliers in the dressing room, most of which depicted the band members wading through blood, with Mike in the lead, each one titled *The Vampire Prospero* in *Rocky Horror Picture Show* font. Come to think of it...Mike did look a little like Tim Curry in all that leather and lace.

I was about to comment on the resemblance when Mike spoke up, "Alright, change of plans, bros. We're gonna drain this bitch before the show. We'll look totally—"

"Creepy?" I offered, again.

"Kill her."

Get the full book ONLINE! *http://www.shaynesilvers.com/l/206897*

MAKE A DIFFERENCE

Reviews are the most powerful tools in my arsenal when it comes to getting attention for my books. Much as I'd like to, I don't have the financial muscle of a New York publisher.

But I do have something much more powerful and effective than that, and it's something that those publishers would kill to get their hands on.

A committed and loyal bunch of readers.

Honest reviews of my books help bring them to the attention of other readers.

If you've enjoyed this book, I would be very grateful if you could spend just five minutes leaving a review on my book's Amazon page.

Thank you very much in advance.

ACKNOWLEDGMENTS

Team Temple and the Den of Freaks on Facebook have become family to me. I couldn't do it without die-hard readers like them.

I would also like to thank you, the reader. I hope you enjoyed reading *ANGEL DUST* as much as I enjoyed writing it. Be sure to check out the two crossover series in the Temple Verse: The **Nate Temple Series** and the **Phantom Queen Diaries**.

And last, but definitely not least, I thank my wife, Lexy. Without your support, none of this would have been possible.

ABOUT SHAYNE SILVERS

Shayne is a man of mystery and power, whose power is exceeded only by his mystery...

He currently writes the Amazon Bestselling **Nate Temple** Series, which features a foul-mouthed wizard from St. Louis. He rides a bloodthirsty unicorn, drinks with Achilles, and is pals with the Four Horsemen.

He also writes the Amazon Bestselling **Feathers and Fire** Series—a second series in the TempleVerse. The story follows a rookie spell-slinger named Callie Penrose who works for the Vatican in Kansas City. Her problem? Hell seems to know more about her past than she does.

He coauthors **The Phantom Queen Diaries**—a third series set in The TempleVerse—with Cameron O'Connell. The story follows Quinn MacKenna, a mouthy black magic arms dealer in Boston. All she wants? A round-trip ticket to the Fae realm...and maybe a drink on the house.

He also writes the **Shade of Devil Series**, which tells the story of Sorin Ambrogio—the world's FIRST vampire. He was put into a magical slumber by a Native American Medicine Man when the Americas were first discovered by Europeans. Sorin wakes up after five-hundred years to learn that his protégé, Dracula, stole his reputation and that no one has ever even heard of Sorin Ambrogio. The streets of New York City will run with blood as Sorin reclaims his legend.

Shayne holds two high-ranking black belts, and can be found writing in a coffee shop, cackling madly into his computer screen while pounding shots of espresso. He's hard at work on the newest books in the TempleVerse— You can find updates on new releases or chronological reading order on the next page, his website, or any of his social media accounts. **Follow him online for all sorts of groovy goodies, giveaways, and new release updates:**

BOOKS BY SHAYNE SILVERS

CHRONOLOGY: All stories in the TempleVerse are shown in chronological order on the following page

FEATHERS AND FIRE SERIES

(Also set in the TempleVerse)

by Shayne Silvers

UNCHAINED

RAGE

WHISPERS

ANGEL'S ROAR

MOTHERLUCKER (Novella #4.5 in the 'LAST CALL' anthology)

SINNER

BLACK SHEEP

GODLESS

ANGHELLIC

TRINITY

HALO BREAKER

ANGEL DUST

NATE TEMPLE SERIES

(Main series in the TempleVerse)

by Shayne Silvers

FAIRY TALE - FREE prequel novella #0 for my subscribers

OBSIDIAN SON

BLOOD DEBTS

GRIMM

SILVER TONGUE

BEAST MASTER

BEERLYMPIAN (Novella #5.5 in the 'LAST CALL' anthology)

TINY GODS

DADDY DUTY (Novella #6.5)

WILD SIDE

WAR HAMMER

NINE SOULS

HORSEMAN

LEGEND

KNIGHTMARE

ASCENSION

CARNAGE

SAVAGE

PHANTOM QUEEN DIARIES

(Also set in the TempleVerse)

by Cameron O'Connell & Shayne Silvers

COLLINS (Prequel novella #0 in the 'LAST CALL' anthology)

WHISKEY GINGER

COSMOPOLITAN

MOTHERLUCKER (Novella #2.5 in the 'LAST CALL' anthology)

OLD FASHIONED

DARK AND STORMY

MOSCOW MULE

WITCHES BREW

SALTY DOG

SEA BREEZE

HURRICANE

BRIMSTONE KISS

MOONSHINE

CHRONOLOGICAL ORDER: TEMPLE VERSE

FAIRY TALE (TEMPLE PREQUEL)

OBSIDIAN SON (TEMPLE 1)

BLOOD DEBTS (TEMPLE 2)

GRIMM (TEMPLE 3)

SILVER TONGUE (TEMPLE 4)

BEAST MASTER (TEMPLE 5)

BEERLYMPIAN (TEMPLE 5.5)

TINY GODS (TEMPLE 6)

DADDY DUTY (TEMPLE NOVELLA 6.5)

UNCHAINED (FEATHERS...1)

RAGE (FEATHERS...2)

WILD SIDE (TEMPLE 7)

WAR HAMMER (TEMPLE 8)

WHISPERS (FEATHERS...3)

COLLINS (PHANTOM 0)

WHISKEY GINGER (PHANTOM...1)

NINE SOULS (TEMPLE 9)

COSMOPOLITAN (PHANTOM...2)

ANGEL'S ROAR (FEATHERS...4)

MOTHERLUCKER (FEATHERS 4.5, PHANTOM 2.5)

OLD FASHIONED (PHANTOM...3)

HORSEMAN (TEMPLE 10)

DARK AND STORMY (PHANTOM...4)

MOSCOW MULE (PHANTOM...5)

SINNER (FEATHERS...5)

WITCHES BREW (PHANTOM...6)

LEGEND (TEMPLE...11)

SALTY DOG (PHANTOM...7)

BLACK SHEEP (FEATHERS...6)

GODLESS (FEATHERS...7)

KNIGHTMARE (TEMPLE 12)

ASCENSION (TEMPLE 13)

SEA BREEZE (PHANTOM...8)

HURRICANE (PHANTOM...9)

BRIMSTONE KISS (PHANTOM...10)

ANGHELLIC (FEATHERS...8)

CARNAGE (TEMPLE 14)

MOONSHINE (PHANTOM...11)

TRINITY (FEATHERS...9)

SAVAGE (TEMPLE...15)

HALO BREAKER (FEATHERS...10)

ANGEL DUST (FEATHERS...11)

SHADE OF DEVIL SERIES

(Not part of the Temple Verse)

by Shayne Silvers

DEVIL'S DREAM

DEVIL'S CRY

DEVIL'S BLOOD

DEVIL'S DUE (_coming 2021..._)

NOTHING TO SEE HERE.

Thanks for reaching the last page of the book, you over-achiever. Sniff the spine. You've earned it. Or sniff your Kindle.

Now this has gotten weird.

Alright. I'm leaving.

Printed in Great Britain
by Amazon

71567745R00113